"What If I Told You That I Believe In Magic?"

Jill asked mischievously.

"I would politely suggest that you were nuts," Grey replied.

At that, Jill walked over to the cupboard and poured a glass of liquid from a brown jug there. "It's just wine. Homemade, as you might expect. I would have offered it to you before, but I thought you would mind."

"You thought I would mind that it was homemade?"

"No, I thought you'd mind that it was violet wine. I already told you that anything made with violets has love potion properties."

"Well, Jill, I want you to see how worried I am." He finished the glass in three gulps. "There's nothing in this wine—or in those potions of yours—that can affect me."

Dear Reader:

Welcome! You hold in your hand a Silhouette Desire—your ticket to a whole new world of reading pleasure.

A Silhouette Desire is a sensuous, contemporary romance about passions, problems and the ultimate power of love. It is about today's woman—intelligent, successful, giving—but it is also the story of a romance between two people who are strong enough to follow their own individual paths, yet strong enough to compromise, as well.

These books are written by, for and about every woman that you are—wife, mother, sister, lover, daughter, career woman. A Silhouette Desire heroine must face the same challenges, achieve the same successes, in her story as you do in your own life.

The Silhouette reader is not afraid to enjoy herself. She knows when to take things seriously and when to indulge in a fantasy world. With six books a month, Silhouette Desire strives to meet her many moods, but each book is always a compelling love story.

Make a commitment to romance—go wild with Silhouette Desire!

Best,

Isabel Swift
Senior Editor & Editorial Coordinator

JENNIFER GREENE
Love Potion

Silhouette Desire

Published by Silhouette Books New York

America's Publisher of Contemporary Romance

SILHOUETTE BOOKS
300 East 42nd St., New York, N.Y. 10017

ISBN: 0-373-05421-1

First Silhouette Books printing May 1988

Books by Jennifer Greene

Silhouette Desire

Body and Soul #263
Foolish Pleasure #293
Madam's Room #326
Dear Reader #350
Minx #366
Lady Be Good #385
Love Potion #421

Silhouette Intimate Moments

Secrets #221

JENNIFER GREENE

lives near Lake Michigan. Born in Grosse Pointe, she moved to a farm when she married her husband fifteen years ago. Jennifer feels that love needs both laughter and tribulations to grow. She's won the *Romantic Times* award for Sensuality and the RWA Silver Medallion, and also writes under the name of Jeanne Grant.

One

When a man gave up, he died.

Grey knew the exact moment when he gave up. The swarm of hornets and the long crashing fall down the ravine had happened hours ago. Now his entire existence was the rocks digging into his spine, the damp black night, the ceaseless rain.

Exhaustion was an old familiar friend, but not like this. No sounds but the steady hiss and spatter of rain intruded in the woods. His clothes were soaked; his skin was soaked. He knew his ankle was broken and that the gash on his temple was swollen and still bleeding. He'd spent a fair amount of time professionally evaluating the extent of his own concussion. It didn't seem to matter any more.

He couldn't move, he wasn't going to get out of here, and all he could hear was the rain. The virgin woods were a shadow world of glistening black stillness. He kept thinking that he'd come a thousand miles for solitude and answers, but somehow he'd always believed the answers would add up to more than this.

Thinking took energy. Lucidity was becoming more and more elusive. Red was the color of pain, and the ocean in his head was stark red and endless. He floated on waves, lost in a fog. It wasn't so bad. Grey hadn't wasted time on dreams in years, but these dreams were potent, wild and as alluring as a man's secret fantasies. In one, he imagined a woman's magical voice and the scents of flowers and spring. Soothing hands reached out to him, and the voice was a low, sultry alto, a whisper of feminine spice.

"Come on, Tiger. Stop fighting me. We've got to get you out of here."

In the dream, he saw eyes as green as a river.

He felt the brush of a woman's soft hair, red-gold, a sleepy tumble of fire.

He heard that nagging voice like the scold of velvet.

Then . . . silence.

Jill had done all she knew how to do. She also knew it wasn't enough. Arms wrapped around her bent knees, she worriedly studied her stranger.

Wolf had taken root by the injured man's bedside, as if claiming possession of the battered loot she'd found in the woods. If the dog hadn't driven her half crazy with her barking and howling, Jill would hardly have been inclined to take a rambling walk through the woods at two o'clock in the morning in a lightning storm.

Every muscle and bone in her body complained that she was of no size to drag a one-hundred-eighty-pound man the distance to the cabin. She also had the sense not to move someone with a head injury, but there had been no other choice. He couldn't be left. She'd managed to get him here. She'd stripped him, she'd splinted the ankle and bandaged his head and treated the welts on his shoulder and chest. The whole time she was dominantly aware how desperately he needed a doctor.

He still did.

And she still had no possible way to get him one.

The sun had risen an hour before. Pale lemon sunshine shimmered through the two open windows, landing on the pine bedpost, the white pillow, his face. He was such a mess. A wrestler after a losing fight couldn't have looked more beaten, and her stranger was no wrestler.

She studied him yet again, helplessly seeking clues as to who he was, where he was from. His body refused to yield her answers. He was built long and lean with broad shoulders. His skin was resilient and sinew dominated his chest and upper arms and thighs, all signs that he was physically fit. So were a zillion men.

His clothes had told her a little about him, but not much. His boots were expensive leather and his shirt carried an affluent label, but not from a store around here. She'd found no wallet in his jeans, but she'd guessed his age at around thirty-five from his face.

She found herself focusing again and again on his face. The bruises and bandages made it difficult to picture what he would normally look like. Night whiskers blurred his square jaw, and his mouth was no more than a slash of white. Another time, though, character lines would obviously dominate his angular features. His brows were straight, his eyelashes short and thick, his nose a blade. She'd thought his hair was brown, but under the sunlight it was more mahogany, rich and thick and dark. He cut it short.

He was a good-looking man, but not in a regular way. His bones were too strong, the composite too austere and bold to label him anything as obvious—or as pale—as "handsome." He had a man's face, not a boy's. He'd seen life. He'd known women. He knew what it was to walk the edge, because the pain lines were not new. She could easily picture his face in a boardroom, a courtroom, even a bedroom.

The only thing she couldn't picture was what on earth he was doing anywhere near her private corner of Tennessee. Hunting squirrel and stringing a line in the Tennessee River for catfish were favorite occupations in the area. He didn't look the type to indulge in either. Although when it came down to it, she didn't care what type he was or what he did for a living.

Jill dragged a hand through her hair. Anxiety dominated every beat of her heart. Most of the time he'd been completely unconscious, but his eyes had opened more than once. She kept looking for answers in his face as to who he was, what had happened to him, how he had come to be in her woods, but it was his eyes that alternately fascinated and frightened her.

He had Abe Lincoln eyes, deep and black and sad. A lost man, a man buried in despair, had eyes like that. They were beautiful eyes, hauntingly dark and empty and full of silent pain. So old. Those eyes were so old.

Dammit, she swore silently. What on earth am I going to do with you, stranger?

He stirred, and she instantly forgot her own exhaustion, lurched out of the rocker and flew over to him. His skin was burning up. The last time she'd tried to spoon tea in his mouth he'd hurled the cup clear across the room. He should have been too weak to fight her, but nightmares seemed to dominate his delirium.

"Shh. Shh. I'm not your enemy, Tiger. Stop fighting me. Nothing's that bad. You're all right, you're all right...."

But she knew he wasn't.

Don't you dare die on me, she begged. Don't you dare.

The clutches of pain were fire-hot red, and the heat was smothering him.

He tasted a hot, foul brew that was somehow familiar.

He felt soothing fingertips on his bare skin.

He heard the magic voice talking, talking, talking.

He smelled the rage of fragrances again. No air was this sweet, no blend of flowers this powerful. None of it was real. The sensations all came from the dream. From her.

It was night when Grey finally opened his eyes. His focus blurred on the glow of a kerosene lamp and walls of rough-cut lodgepole pine. The room was square, with two shuttered windows and a bare wood floor. Strange-looking branches hung in clusters from the beamed ceiling. The dresser was ancient, hand-carved and scarred. He'd never seen any of it before.

Heat still blanketed his body. Pain snapped at his skin like a yapping hound's teeth. His vision refused to completely clear. Thinking hurt. Hell, breathing hurt.

Mentally he tried to catalog what he knew, what he was sure of. The pain was logical. Bandages seemed to be in place where bandages were supposed to be. For the first time he understood shock and concussion, not as symptoms leading to a diagnosis, but as sensations. Annoying sensations. Weakness. Heat. Dizziness.

All of that was expected, logical, reasonable. He knew he was hurt, but he didn't know what had happened to the rain. His mind annoyingly wanted to hover between dream and reality. He could smell woods and earth and that whole fog of thick sweet scents—where did they *come* from? And then he forgot the smells.

The rug on the bare wood floor moved, and turned into a rangy gray-brown beast that looked like a wolf. Limpid eyes stared at Grey. He ignored them. The rocker in the far corner was occupied.

She didn't much look like the kind of woman who could haunt a man.

The lady was barefoot, and her legs were thrown over the rocker arm. She seemed to be wearing a huge red shirt and nothing else. Mites were bigger. She was folded up in the rocker with room to spare, and her hair was an unbrushed tumble that shadowed small-boned features—a wisp of a mouth, a delicate arch of brows, fragile cheekbones. Her skin had the kiss of a glow from the lamplight and freckles sprayed across her nose.

He could have sworn she was dead asleep, yet he barely blinked and suddenly those endless green eyes focused on him.

"Hi, Tiger."

He knew the voice. He even knew her smile—soft, slow and immediate. She climbed out of the rocker in one smooth, graceful motion and moved toward him.

"You're hurting, I know. Don't try to talk yet."

Two of her fingers pressed on the inside of his wrist. He felt her other palm on his forehead, cool and soothing, soft. He was aware of being buck naked under the white sheet. He was aware of being alive. Because of her.

"I've been calling you Tiger for two days now, simply because I didn't have any other name and it seemed to fit. You're quite a fighter, aren't you? And

I don't mind telling you that you've given me one heck of a time."

She turned away from him for a minute, but she never stopped talking. He'd have given up everything except for that voice. When nothing else had been real, he'd held on to the sound of her. Suddenly it wasn't that easy to accept that she was real—that she was just a woman, a barefoot lady in red cotton with green eyes like a river.

"Disorienting to wake up in a strange place, isn't it? And I'll answer everything I can think of so you won't have to talk. I'm Jill Stanton—I told you that, but I'll bet you don't remember. This is my cabin; my dog found you in the storm. I have no idea where you were headed for, but you found a good stretch of Tennessee woods to get lost in. I figured you were traveling by river—you almost had to be. The fastest way to get to a town is by boat, and cars aren't much use around here. We're not even on a map. Yes, I know you hate this taste but it'll make you feel better. Just a sip. Black willow has the same salicylic-acid base as aspirin. It's the nearest thing I have to a pain reliever; we have to get that fever down."

While she talked, her arm sneaked around his neck. Her shoulder supported his head as she forced the cup to his lips. He knew she'd done it before. He even had a vague memory of batting a cup out of her hands, but other things were more familiar. The drift of her hair catching the light, the shadow of her breasts when she bent over him, the knife stab in his head when he tried to move, the sweet, sensual scent of her. Above and beyond that, nothing could conceivably taste more bitter, more foul or more vile than the dark liquid sneaking down his throat.

"Come on, one more sip. I swear to heavens if you fight me this time, I'm going to have Wolf sit on you."

Once he swallowed, she took the cup away and her arm slid out from beneath him. She leaned away. He heard water being wrung from a cloth. It wasn't cold, but it felt like a splash of ice when she gently applied it to his forehead, his cheeks, his throat. The whole time she kept talking to him in that slow, soothing alto, answering the dozen questions he couldn't find the strength to ask.

"I'll tell you something, Tiger. You were really no beauty when I ran into you. The gash on your forehead was a gem, and you had to pick the rockiest ravine in Tennessee to fall down, didn't you? I taped your ankle and strapped it with a wooden cast like the pioneers used to wear—it looks pretty crude, but it works. The break looked simple and clean; your leg's swollen some but not badly, which is more than I can say for the welts on your chest and arms. What'd you do, walk right into a hornets' nest? You must have smelled the honey, which is exactly what your upper body is smothered in. Honey's not only a natural antibiotic, but it has antihistamine properties. My best guess is that you could use some massive doses of both, pharmacy-style, but a little basic first aid wasn't going to wait."

When she was done with the cloth, she peeled the sheet down to his waist. He couldn't stop staring at

her. Her small, smooth hands efficiently removed the
bandages from his chest and shoulders. Like she said,
he could smell honey, but the fresh compresses she laid
on his chest were something different, something
warm, stinging, drying.

He paid little attention. He'd already identified,
evaluated and dismissed the same injuries she'd described. His whole body felt whipped and battered,
but professional instincts would have warned him if
there was any pain he shouldn't have expected.

The woman troubled him more. She'd disturbed
him in those dreams, and she was still disturbing him.
He wasn't sure why. She certainly wasn't beautiful.
Her mouth was too small. The red shirt fit her like a
man's shirt, huge and bulky.

She had power in her voice and hands that didn't
connect with the picture of a small, fragile woman,
and her talk of black willow and honey and antihis-
tamines made him think of white witches and fake
healers. Mystical nonsense. Tiny cloisonné rainbows
dangled from her ears. The whimsical earrings suited
her. Whimsy suited Grey not at all, and neither did
feeling helpless, mesmerized by a sprite of a woman he
didn't know or want to know. And the rage of aching
pain kept swimming in his head.

"If I'd had a way to get you to a doctor, I would
have, but we're not exactly in a metropolis. We're
talking miles of rough backwoods to the nearest clinic,
and trees and branches were down everywhere because of the storm. The obvious choice I had was to
take you by boat into Raider's Cove, but the storm

stole that option away from us, too. I've been practically telling you on the hour that you're fine, on the mend."

Her voice never lost its soothing quality, its sensual magic, but he saw the lights of humor gradually fade from her green eyes. Anxiety, invisible before, darkened her eyes with stress. "Damn it, you're not fine! I have to get you to a doctor, but I simply don't know how I can. The roads are still out. I managed to drag you in from the woods by putting together a travois, but I'll never be able to pull you as far as my dock that way. It's simply too far. Neighbors will be by; then they can help me. I know you must have people looking for you, worried about you, but I..."

"Jill." His voice sounded rusty, and his throat felt like a bedful of nails. That horrible brew of hers was working. He found the strength to circle her wrist with his hand. "I don't want or need a doctor. I do need..."

She frowned, leaning closer. "What?"

"A bathroom."

She nodded casually. "Not to worry. I have a pail right under the bed." When she leaned over, he grabbed her hand again.

"I'm getting up." He knew he was weak, and he knew nausea would hit him the instant he tried to stand. He also knew there wasn't a chance on earth he was using any pail.

"Look, Tiger. I'm twenty-eight years old, I've seen it all before. Let's not get silly, okay?"

"I'm getting up," he repeated. Reality was simply a matter of control. If the concussion were worse, his vision would still be blurred. It wasn't, and he could feel the straps of smooth, carved wood taped securely around his ankle. Moving was simply a matter of will.

He believed that until he lurched up on one elbow. Stars danced in front of his eyes. When he pushed up farther, his forehead turned into a dripping faucet and his one white witch became two. Nausea filled his throat. It felt as if someone was splitting his head with an ax.

"Look, Tiger. Maybe we could show off all this masculine pride tomorrow," she said delicately.

"You *could* help me."

"I am helping you."

"You're just standing there."

She said patiently, "I spent hours putting you back together. I don't want to have to do it again. Who do you think is going to have to repatch and rebandage when you fall flat on your face?"

She might have a voice like magic, she might have sexy green eyes, she might have a bare white throat that could make even a sick man look twice. But at the moment he didn't like her very much.

A few moments later she was tucking the cool sheet around his chin again. "That wasn't so bad now, was it?"

It was. He couldn't count the number of naked bodies he'd seen over the years. He'd never had a high tolerance for a patient's modesty. Illogical, irrational character traits like modesty slowed down the whole process of getting the honest, fast, critical answers integral to healing and health. Only the whole business was different when it was turned against him. He hated being helpless. He hated being dependent.

Maybe he wasn't a doctor any more, but he was unwilling to be a patient.

"You don't accept help very easily, do you, Tiger?" she murmured dryly. "Funny, but I haven't met anyone who didn't need a little help from time to time."

He closed his eyes, trying to ignore her. If the sick feeling didn't pass soon, he was going to disgrace himself. "The name is not Tiger. It's Grey. Grey Treveran."

"Well, Grey Treveran, one way or another I'm going to get you to a doctor," she said softly.

"No, no doctor."

She hesitated, staring down at him with a perplexed frown. "Look, I have some sound first-aid skills, but I never pretended to more. You need some serious, qualified help. Someone who knows what they're doing."

"No doctor." Explaining took too much effort, even if he were willing. He wasn't willing. The emptiness was already rushing back at him. Too much life, too much death. Everything he'd always worked for, believed in, was all gone. The hollowness inside him was like a huge, dark and empty pit. "Please," he whispered to her. "Just leave me alone. I'll be out of your way as soon as I can. One more day. I'll pay you for the trouble."

"Don't insult me, Treveran. Money isn't the problem, but . . ." Jill hesitated, staring at him in silence with the lamplight behind her. She couldn't stop looking at his wild, dark, bleak eyes. What kind of hell did he live in? Turning, she snuffed out the wick's flame and moved toward the door. "We'll talk about it tomorrow, all right? We'll see if your fever's down by morning. In the meantime, I'm in the next room and Wolf won't leave your side. You try to get out of bed alone, and she'll not only fetch me, but you'll be in more trouble than you ever dreamed of. You got that?"

He said nothing. He was already asleep.

The afternoon was sultry and still and far too hot to build a fire inside. A branch cradled between crisscrossed logs made a place for Jill to hang her hook. The wrought-iron pot was suspended over a bed of coals in the shade of a giant sycamore. She stirred the thick brew with a wooden spoon.

It smelled wonderful, although the scents of coconut oil and wood ash would completely evaporate before the brew was finished. Chamomile was the strongest smell, as it should be, with just a hint of orange spice. Jill had had problems with the whole recipe until she'd discovered the proper zinc catalyst.

Making soap the old-fashioned way—the right way—took time. Mosquitoes buzzed in her herb garden. Prickly heat itched behind her knees. The last of the blue violets carpeted the woods in the distance; wild pansies were starting to come up. The hot sun simmered all the smells and colors together, and the result was magic. Water, hills, woods, peace.

She straightened, arching her back to chase away the kinks. She'd arrived at her great-grandmother's cabin three months ago, looking for nothing more than a place to curl up until the hurts disappeared. Now she felt whole, vibrant, zinging with confidence and purpose. Atlanta seemed a million miles away. She hadn't thought of Michael in weeks.

Her gaze darted to the cabin for the dozenth time in the past hour, then wandered back to her local visitor. "Want another glass of lemonade?"

"I tole you a hundred times, Jill. Ain't no need to fuss over me."

She grinned, stirred her mixture one last time, and ambled over to her neighbor. She flopped down on her back with her arms behind her head, taking care to locate upwind of Root. He wasn't much of a man for baths, and as if it weren't a hundred and two in the shade, he wore an old felt hat, flannels and overalls. She'd never seen him dressed any other way.

If anyone had told her three months ago that she'd make friends with a half wild, illiterate, definitely not aromatic mountain man, she wouldn't have believed it. Root was about five foot four, built like wire, and from his grizzly beard to his shotgun he might as well have stepped out of another century. He'd never seen a dentist, never paid a penny of income tax, never owned a television or wanted one.

"Yer soap goin' okay?" he asked her lazily.

"Fine. I've got an order for a hundred and fifty cakes of chamomile due in Nashville next week. That's a long way from competition for Caswell Massey but it'll buy a few groceries." She closed her eyes, smelling the grass and trees—and listening. She knew Wolf would howl the minute Grey wakened, but she still listened. "I've got another order from a place in Chatanooga."

"See? I tole yer you jes had to give it time, and I ain't never heard of that Caswell. My best guess is your stuff is better anyhow."

"They're Gran's recipes, not mine." She opened one eye. Root was settled against the trunk of the sycamore, a pipe in his hand. He'd told her before, it took a good fifty years to properly break in a good pipe. "You might as well tell me what's on your mind. Or did you just hike three miles for my lemonade?"

"I check on you most days. Me or Billy."

"But you don't hang around with a gleam in your eyes most days."

"Locusts are buzzing," he said repressively. "Means a hot dry spell coming up."

"Hmm."

"Maybe I dug up a little news about your stranger. And then maybe I didn't." His lips firmed in a satisfied line when Jill immediately sat up. "Heard there was a boat drifting in Cule's Cove. A houseboat, like they rent around the Land Between the Lakes."

"That's a zillion miles downstream from here."

"I ain't saying it's not. I jes sayin' there's a boat that seems to belong to no one. Horace Stewart happened onto it. He told Marylee Curtis, who told me. Seems Horace took a little sojourn around that boat. Passed on something he thought you might want to take a look at."

Jill picked up the wallet he handed her. She didn't ask if anyone had made any effort to report the lost boat to the authorities. No one else would have, and Root would never.

The wallet was made of fine hand-tooled leather, and held a pile of credit cards, a driver's license for one Grey Treveran and a crease of untouched bills. Root would have starved before touching another man's money. Her fingers lingered on the license. She noted the Chicago address and his age—thirty-four—but was more interested in the license picture.

She'd never met anybody who liked the photo on their driver's license. The pictures always seemed to be taken by sick cameras. This one, though, could well have been a different man. She recognized the short, thick mahogany hair, the strong angular bones. It was definitely Grey, but a Grey with a lazy, easy smile. The tilt of his head spoke of intelligence and confidence and authority. His eyes were snapping black and alive.

The last time she'd seen those eyes, they'd been haunted and lost and empty.

"Well? Is it his?"

"Yes."

Root nodded and went back to packing his pipe. "I suppose Billy and me could manage to get the boat towed in your dock over the next day or so."

"It would help. All he has in the way of clothes is what I found him in, and rags are in better shape than they are."

"So now at least you know for sure who he is."

"I knew that before," she reminded him.

He shook his head. "You knew what he told you before. From what you said, he don't talk about himself, don't tell you where he's from, don't want you to contact nobody. Adds up to a man in trouble any day of this week. He's best out of your hair."

"Yes." A fretful breeze curled a strand of hair around her cheeks. She smoothed it away.

"Three days since you found him now."

"Almost."

Root eyed her shrewdly. "You ain't much on turning people away from your door. But he ain't hills people, Jill. Maybe he's too sick to move now, but he won't be. Yer alone, and you got no reason to trust him."

"No," Jill agreed.

He leaned forward on his haunches. "When I was a kid, I took in a stray lynx cub whose mother was kilt. Ain't no more lynx in these parts, but there was forty years ago. Anyhows, that cub had a thorn in its paw, all festered up. I fixed the critter up, fed it, slept it by my fire. You know what happened?"

"No."

"Bit my finger clear to the bone." Root looked at her meaningfully. "There's a message in that, if yer listening."

"I'm not."

"Didn't think you were. Some days I wonder why I bother talking to you." Root stretched, sighed and was gone. Typical of him, he never wasted a goodbye before fading into the woods again.

Slowly she uncurled from the ground and returned to her pot. A cloud chased across the sun. The day was still bright but also suddenly muted, like her mood. She could feel the weight and bulk of Grey's wallet in her back pocket as she stirred her soap mixture.

Root was right, of course. She had no reason to trust Grey. She had no time or desire to wait on a stranger hand and foot. And he needed a doctor, not a lady with a little background in survival first aid.

Gran had been known as a healer in these backwoods, and Jill had spent her childhood summers being drilled in the use of healing herbs. Root claimed she had "the touch," which was worth about as much as popcorn. She had a background in nutrition. That had no relationship to formal medical education and the label "healer" made her cringe. It reeked of quack medicine and fake cures.

The man laid up in her cabin needed the kind of qualified help she had no way to give him, but Jill felt caught like a fly in a spiderweb. The wallet had only raised more questions than it answered. Grey had money and an affluent address, yet a successful, intelligent, educated man shouldn't be violently opposed to seeing a doctor. He should be worried about his business, and someone—a wife, a woman—should have been desperately worried about him.

Only he seemed to have no one. And worse than that, he didn't seem to care.

He's not your problem, Jill, she mentally reminded herself. But her mind had been feeding her that litany for three days. It didn't seem to do any good. She pushed her hair back, propped her hand on her hip.

These woods had given her back so much. She hadn't come here by choice. She'd come here because she had nowhere else to go where her ex-husband couldn't find her. Michael wasn't too pleased with the divorce decree, and on his third martini Michael generally went looking for someone to bat around.

The marriage had lasted three years. The first year had been wonderful, the last hell. It had taken her longer than it should have to believe that Michael wasn't the same man she had married, that she was not responsible for his drinking problem, and that nothing she did was ever going to help him. It still hurt. It still ached. To walk away from a man she'd once loved heart and soul was the hardest thing she'd ever done. Michael was never evil, just sick. The vows she'd taken in the marriage ceremony were supposed to mean something. What kind of woman would turn away a man who desperately needed help?

Only the last time he'd come to her for help, she'd somehow been the one who'd ended up in a hospital.

She quickly dismissed the painful memories and concentrated on what mattered. Coming here had been the best decision she'd ever made. A stranger viewing the countryside would undoubtedly see nothing more than wild woods and rocky hills and weeds.

The stark poverty of the area was appallingly real; so was the superstition and illiteracy. Places like this weren't supposed to exist, not any more, not in this country.

But they did. And pride came in all forms, which was something Jill had had to learn. The people here had taught her that and maybe so had the woods. Her gaze drifted a distance away. Few plants were as straggly or scaly as coltsfoot. Tansy was another weed that grew angular and tough. Mallow had an ugly hairy stem. Common yarrow and sweet flag and the sow thistle—all of them were nothing but weeds. Each of them had the capacity to heal and do good, if one knew how to use them.

Root had the neighbors believing she knew magic, which annoyed Jill no end. She knew nothing except that there was a time when a woman had to walk away and a time when a woman had to take a stand. The right to care had become her source of strength. The right to grow and change and try again had become her source of pride.

Her head snapped around at Wolf's high-pitched bark inside the cabin. Her unwilling "patient" was awake. He was also undoubtedly going to be crabby, taciturn and difficult. Her stranger wanted nothing more than to be left alone. Given that he couldn't walk two steps without wobbling, that she was worried to death about his continued fever, and that she had no time for this nonsense of baby-sitting a stranger, she hadn't been doing too good a job of leaving him alone.

She zipped toward the porch steps with the shadow of a frown on her forehead. She would have been delighted to kick Grey out her door if he'd had a place to go and someone to watch over him. She'd tell him to leave if she believed he were in shape to take care of himself, but what troubled her most about Treveran of the sad Abe Lincoln eyes was that he was alone.

All he seemed to have was her.

Two

The only thing Grey had to do all day was sleep and examine his injuries. The broken ankle was minor, and all he had to do to reduce the swelling was keep the limb raised. Lying still was the obvious way to ease the symptoms of his concussion. The bee stings were the source of his continued fever—he'd inherited an allergy to bee venom. The fever wasn't dangerous, just nothing to dance around with.

Grey was uniquely qualified to judge that his healing was dependent on little more than solid time and rest.

His professional judgment died at four in the afternoon. He'd had it with time and rest. He'd had it with the fever and the headache. And he'd definitely had it with lying in bed staring at the weeds hanging from the ceiling. He'd smelled all the womanish flowers and herb smells he needed to smell in this lifetime.

The dog perked up when he ripped the honey poultices off his chest. She raised up on all fours when Grey reached for his jeans. The jeans were more shredded holes than cover, but they were better than being naked. Even though Jill had cut off one leg at the knee, it took him what seemed like half a year to wriggle into them. By the time he had the snap buttoned, his head was swimming and his forehead was wet.

He used the bedpost to help himself stand, which was when the gray beast started to get nasty. Her first snarl was low. Teeth bared, ears flat, she let out a second, louder growl.

Knuckles white on the bedpost, he glared at her and waited for the floor to stop rolling. He wasn't ready to take a step, but the dog didn't seem to know that. She started a series of high-pitched, frantic yips that splintered shards of pain in his head.

He hadn't blinked twice before Jill was standing in the doorway. All Jill ever had to do was appear and the raging wolf-beast turned back into a whining mongrel. As fast as Jill petted her, the mutt groaned and moaned as if tattletale reporting everything Grey had just done.

"Would you mind calling off your familiar?" Grey asked.

"I keep telling you she's just showing off. The only thing she ever bites is mosquitoes."

"She hates me."

"She's adopted you," Jill corrected.

He felt the swift, assessing sweep of her eyes and braced himself. They'd already argued that morning about the stitches he wasn't going to have for the gash in his forehead. She'd called him a pigheaded idiot and kissed his cheek like he was four years old. God knew what kind of fuss she was going to raise over taking off her sticky poultices.

He hadn't figured out Jill yet. How does a man figure out a woman dressed in wild apricot jeans and a top that looked like underwear? Her hair was a mess and her freckles had a sunburn. Privacy wasn't in her vocabulary. She was a terribly upsetting woman, the walls refused to stop spinning, and expecting an argument, he warily noticed her sudden smile.

"So I see we're determined to get up and even dressed for dinner?" Jill perched her hands on her hips. "Well? You feel like climbing mountains or just swimming the English Channel?"

"Don't give me a hard time. I'm getting out of this room or die trying. I've laid in that bed all I'm going to lay in bed."

She nodded. If he had been four years old, she could have spanked him. He belonged in bed. She could see the peppered welts on his chest, the ash color of fever in his face, his white-knuckled hold on the bedpost. She could also smell mutiny in the air if she didn't agree. "Okay. The three of us can try a short excursion to the kitchen."

"I can do it alone."

He couldn't, of course. Three hobbling steps and his teeth clamped together and his lips turned white. She moved in and under his shoulder, wrapping her arm tight around his bare waist. His skin was so smooth and warm she felt a bolt of awareness. Even battered, Grey was a potent male package. More relevant was making sure she didn't press against his bruises or cuts.

"I can—"

"Oh, shut up, Treveran. We both know I love getting my hands on your body, so just humor me." As she edged with him through the open doorway, she peeked at his face. She could tell he didn't want to, but his mouth was starting to curl in a reluctant smile. "If you're really good," she continued, "I might even make you a cup of tea."

"God. No, thank you."

She chuckled. "One would think you didn't like my herbal brews," she said sadly, but then she stopped trying to talk. Supporting his weight took all her energy and Grey hobbled so slowly.

After they entered the kitchen, she settled him in the high-back rocker by the west window and placed a stool under his ankle before he could protest. She told him about his boat and his wallet while she dampened a cloth under the water pump.

She was sure the news of his boat would have interested him. It didn't, nor did he once glance at his wallet. All he did was bat at her hand when she tried to wipe his forehead. She ignored him, smoothing the cool cloth on his temples and neck.

"You're a bully, Jill," he said wearily.

"It's lust, I keep telling you. I just can't keep my hands off you."

"You're also more full of sass than any ten women I ever met." His head leaned back, eyes shuttered at exhausted half-mast. "I've never felt this weak in my entire life, and I don't like being so much trouble to you. You don't need a stranger in your way like this."

She nodded. "Keep feeling guilty about it, Treveran," she suggested gravely.

He opened his mouth and then closed it as he became aware of his surroundings. She wanted to think he noticed the charm, but his expression suggested that he was something more like appalled.

Amused, she watched his gaze pounce from spot to spot. The dry sink and water pump were a hundred years old, and so was the knotted pine table. Drying herbs hung from the open rafters, and sweet flag was strewn on the wood floor. Pioneer style, the oven was built into the brick hearth. Woven baskets were full of roots, and the scents dominating the room—violets and ginger, cinnamon and wild tansy—were overpoweringly old-fashioned.

He looked from corner to corner, and then leveled a patient, "No electricity?"

"Nope."

"No refrigeration?"

"I have a well pit to keep things cool, and at this time of year I pretty much cook outside. Too hot for a fire in here. There's a rabbit stew simmering just outside the window, when you're hungry."

"I see."

He didn't, she knew. He motioned to the trays on the table. "What are those?"

"Soap molds."

"I see," he said again, and brushed a hand over his face.

It wasn't the first time she'd seen a vague uneasiness steal over Grey's features. She seemed to regularly bother him, which struck her as humorous. She was just a woman—no special mysteries, no special fascinations—but letting him think otherwise had turned into a full-time hobby. Left alone, he'd stare at a window and brood. Teasing him had become the only way she knew to erase the cold, haunted emptiness in his eyes.

"You live here. Like this," he said slowly.

He worked hard to keep any judgmental values out of his tone, but a bit escaped. Her tone was blithe and easy. "Sure do. About a hundred years ago, the cabin was built Tennessee dogtrot style, which means that the rooms lead off of an open outside hallway. I think the original idea was to promote airflow during these hot summer days, but the outside hall makes rainy and windy days rather interesting." He wasn't listening. He was too busy warily studying the glass of clear liquid she set in front of him. "Don't panic. It's just water."

He took a testing sip. "Do you," he asked carefully, "do anything in particular to make a living?"

"Slowly but surely I'm trying to build up a mail-order business selling herbal cosmetics. Soaps, lotions, scents, that kind of thing." She would have let it go at that. Maybe because something finally sparked in his eyes besides emptiness, she simply couldn't. "My neighbors would also tell you that I make love potions. Practice a little white witchcraft. I don't suppose you believe in that kind of thing?"

"No." His eyes announced he didn't believe her, but he very carefully said nothing.

She swallowed a smile, and silence reigned in the kitchen while she let him worry about it. The rabbit stew had been simmering with spring-sweet peas. She served it with wild rice. He might have eaten more if he'd been less busy stealing glances at her face. She gave him a little more to think about when, after dinner, she carted in the giant pot from outside. He watched her ladle the soap mixture into the molds—a long, tedious job that took more than an hour.

By the time the molds were full and left to cool on the hearth, it was time to light a lamp. Night shimmered in on a wave of sweet smells. Evening primrose and bouncing bet and dame's rocket surrounded the cabin; all of their flowering scents exploded at night. Smells and shadows flickered through the small room like magic.

Grey wasn't much of a man for magic. When he spoke again, it was obvious what was on his mind. "You don't really do that."

"What?"

"Make love potions."

"I certainly do." She shook out the match and remounted the hurricane glass over the oil lamp.

Straightening, she shot him a critical glance. "You're beginning to look as wild as Root with that five-day-old beard, Treveran. You want me to take care of it for you, or are you ready to go back in the bedroom and crash?"

He ignored the question. "You're an intelligent woman. Not the kind to believe in hocus-pocus."

"Hmm." She found towels and dampened them, the best she could do to soften his beard. The cabin didn't stock shaving cream.

"You're living here like out of the dark ages."

She draped the damp towels on his cheeks like an old-fashioned barber, and then sharpened the straight razor on a leather strop. "My gran lived the same way. This was her cabin. I spent half my childhood here," she told him conversationally. "Gran had a big reputation for being a healer—"

Grey didn't want to hear about her grandmother. "You haven't always lived here, then."

She adjusted one lamp, then moved another one closer. "I'm from Atlanta. I worked as a nutritionist for the Atlanta Tropical Disease Control Center for five years. My parents still live in the city, and I have a brother in Arizona. Tilt your face up, will you?"

"You're not married?"

She hesitated. "Not now."

"But you were."

"Shh." Shadows darkened every corner of the room. All the light was on his face, throat and shoulders. He stared at her with his dark eyes when she removed the first towel and edged between his legs. He

braced his thighs as she bent over and applied the
blade to his cheek.

Her light mood suddenly hovered like a spring
breeze, unstable, fretful, elusive. It wasn't that she
minded his questions. The opposite was true, she was
relieved to see life in his face, emotion, reaction. If she
thought it would have earned a full-blooded smile out
of him, she would happily have turned cartwheels.

She just wished he hadn't brought marriage into the
conversation. Perhaps that wouldn't have mattered if
the act of shaving a man were less personal, less intimate, less . . . close.

A shiver skidded up her spine, like a ghost had just
stepped on her shadow. The feel of Grey's iron thighs
tensing against her induced a silly, uneasy beat to her
heart. Her palms dampened annoyingly.

"What's wrong?" he asked quietly.

"Nothing. Just trying to find the best angle." She
smiled at him. She also moved away. Once the whiskers were gone under his nose and chin, she could
reach him just as easily from the side. "If I were a
man, I'd grow a beard. This is awful. I can't imagine
how men do this every day without cutting themselves."

"Jill."

"What?"

"Could you try and be a little more reassuring while
you have a straight blade in your hand?" he added.
"I'm still not sure how I got myself into this. I can
shave myself."

She chuckled. "Believe me, you'll have the job back once your fever's gone. For now, I'm tired of cleaning up nicks and scratches on you, Treveran."

She removed the last towel, dipped the blade in water and braced her free palm on his jaw when she tackled the area around his sideburns. His flesh was warm. The lamplight gleamed on his bare chest, and her heart kept going click click click like a pistol being cocked over and over again.

For heaven's sake, Jill, she chided herself.

But it was night, and she was completely isolated with a man she barely knew, so perhaps a slight awareness of her own vulnerability was justified. She'd never handled feelings of vulnerability well. Helplessness had always colored her worse nightmares. But Grey was not Michael, she reminded herself.

She'd also told herself a hundred times that fear had nothing to do with her feelings for her ex-husband. Whenever she remembered Michael, she tried to recall the best of the man she had first fallen in love with—the winsome grin, the dance in his eyes, his ability to find laughter in everything. To dwell on her last memories of her ex-husband was pointless. Michael had made his own hell. In the end he'd been incapable of being responsible for his own actions. And she was over every trauma Michael had put her through. Completely.

Grey's fingers suddenly circled her wrist, startling her. "If I upset you asking questions, I apologize," he said quietly.

He immediately released his hand. Jill decided the
odd anxiety was only in her head, so she banished it.
"I can't imagine where you got that idea. There isn't
a question on earth you could ask that would upset
me," she assured him lightly.

That was true, she discovered as she became intimately acquainted with his throat and chin over the
next few minutes. The differences between Grey and
Michael couldn't have been more obvious. Grey was
built lean, tall, strong. His hair was thick, dark. The
lines of his face mapped integrity and honesty. If she
really had to pinpoint the difference between Michael
and Grey, it was that Grey was a man in a way Michael had never managed to be.

She drew back, critically studying the results of her
shaving. The face was fine, but soon—very soon—she
was going to have to do something about his eyes.
Grey did an outstanding job of denying pain but his
deep black eyes still told her stories about dreams lost,
illusions destroyed, and passion. It was the passion
that kept drawing her. Shallow people suffered shallow hurts. Whatever had happened in Grey's life
caused him to ache from the soul.

"That bad?" he asked with a trace of impatience.

"Bad? You have to be kidding. I've just turned you
back into a hopelessly handsome brute again, Treveran." She whisked away the towels. "Want a mirror
to see how you look?"

Grey didn't answer her. In part, the effort of staying upright for these few hours had drained him more

than he wanted to believe. In part, he simply couldn't take his eyes off Jill.

She was a mystery, and Grey wasn't fond of mysteries. The whimsical and fanciful bothered him— anything less than reality had always bothered him. Illusions and fantasies were words for fairy tales. And it seemed to him that nine parts out of ten of Jill were clear-cut, unfathomable nonsense.

Her green eyes were full of the devil and her smile was cheeky. She was full of contradictions. Barefoot women shouldn't regularly read the *Wall Street Journal*. A woman with an education and valuable career should hardly be choosing to live as rustic as a pioneer. She knew something about real health care— damn it, she'd practically brought him back from the dead—but she talked up love potions. She had absolutely no self-consciousness about bodies. Heaven knew, she hadn't honored any privacy about his, and she swished that small fanny of hers around like a woman who enjoyed being a woman.

But for a few seconds' span when she'd been shaving him, he'd seen something in her eyes. An awareness, a wariness, a tug of something nameless that had upset her.

Leave it alone, Treveran. It's her business, and you're in no position to care, he thought.

"Hey, where's my thank-you?" Jill demanded lightly. "You look adorable thanks to me, Treveran."

"Thank you." The words were empty.

So were his eyes. Jill draped the towels on a rack to dry, put away the razor, and then determinedly walked over to him. The disturbing sexual vibrations had disappeared, or maybe her heart had simply accepted those feelings for the foolishness they were. Grey wasn't going to hurt anyone. He was the one who was hurt, not just outside, but inside, too. The look in his eyes tore at her.

She leaned over and gently, softly pressed her lips on his. It was both less than a kiss and more. There was a certain type of intimacy that has nothing to do with nakedness and this was it. His lips were cool and smooth. He tasted fresh. He also tasted like a man who would make a powerful, unforgettable lover, but if that thought raised intricate shadows for Jill she ignored them.

He never moved. His body went silent and still; his mouth neither gave nor took nor responded to the touch of hers. She offered. A promise of emotion, the flavor of something sweet, the lure of magic. He would have her believe he felt nothing at all, but when she raised her head she could see healthy color flooding his face.

"Don't."

The word was clipped. She'd reached him. He felt—but he didn't want to.

"Leave me alone, Jill." He didn't know how to say it any stronger, any plainer, any clearer.

She finished setting the kitchen to rights for the night, and then systematically turned down each oil lamp. When the room was in darkness, she whispered, "No."

* * *

He was in trouble with her again. Grey leaned against the bark of the whitewood and closed his eyes until the disgusting feeling of weakness passed.

Jill was a hundred yards away, wearing indecently short shorts and a sleeveless red shirt, hoeing in the hot sun. What she was hoeing for, he had no idea. Her whole garden wasl weeds, and it was too big for her to handle alone. When he'd awakened that morning, he was fed up with watching her carry heavy pots and heaving buckets of water around and hoeing that monster garden alone.

Since she wouldn't take money for taking care of him, and Grey knew damn well he couldn't cope without help for a little time yet, he decided to help her.

He'd tried carrying out a heavy pot for her and had fallen flat on his face. That was when she'd taken away his cane, stashed him in the shade of the whitewood, and sicced the beast on him. Grey's eyes opened irritably on the mangy gray critter at his feet. The dog never slept. She just stared at him with those limpid black eyes, daring him to move.

"One of these days, you and I are going to have to come to terms. You don't really think you have me fooled, do you? You're not going to bite."

Wolf thumped her tail. Grey leaned forward and the dog lurched up on all fours and growled.

"Dogs like me. Cats like me. Damn it, kids have always liked me. Why don't you?" he added wearily.

"You do everything she tells you to, that's your problem. She's got you bewitched."

He leaned back again, ignored the dog and watched Jill. The woods were cool and still behind him. The day was a Tennessee stinger, sultry and close. Insects hummed in the jungle of wildflowers that bordered the woods. She had a black iron pot suspended over a bed of coals in the distance. She was cooking comfrey, she'd told him. He'd mentally shaken his head.

A mug was on a basket tray within his reach. Ox-eyed daisy tea. It sounded pretty. It tasted putrid. She claimed it would calm him down. To his thorough irritation, he discovered it did.

As it happened, he needed to calm down. He'd been in the kitchen when she'd had a visitor that morning, a young girl named Sally. She'd been dressed in century-old hand-me-downs, was missing a front tooth and had been shredding a hankie as she whispered to Jill. There was a boy over on Beaver Ridge. She'd wanted Jill to give her some periwinkle leaves to attract him.

Jill had actually given them to her. Serious as you please, she'd fixed up this whole packet of silly leaves and given them to the girl. He still didn't believe it.

His eyes narrowed irritably on her slim figure in the weed patch. He'd seen plenty of life. Eccentrics came in all styles, ages and shapes, but darn it, Jill wasn't eccentric. She was normal. Regular. Healthy, sassy, smart, funny. Natural. Her hair was always a mess. She swore when a mosquito nailed her and she had freckles on her nose. She was too real to be eccentric.

She was too smart to have dropped out of life to hide away in the woods growing weeds for a living.

She was too damn beautiful to be living alone.

I'm tired of thinking about you, Jill Stanton. You're driving me nuts. Leave me alone...

When he opened his eyes the next time, the shadows had lengthened; the birds had stopped chirping in the late afternoon heat and Jill was no longer in her garden. She was standing in the shadow of her porch and she had company.

The old codger had visited her yesterday and Grey recognized him as the man she called Root. The other man was unfamiliar. He was built heavy and round, with squinty blue eyes and a twelve-inch neck. Jill and Root were standing. The stranger was laid back against her porch steps, his head thrown back and his teeth clamped together.

The porch overhang was shadowed so Grey couldn't see much. He didn't need to see much to recognize a man in pain. Lightning fast, he felt old instincts surge through him—the need to look, assess, evaluate, treat, help.

He had to lock like a steel wall against the tree to keep from moving. The man was none of his business. Doctoring was not his business. Not now. Maybe not ever again.

The summer rental of the houseboat had represented the first vacation he'd taken in seven years. It also represented time he had to have. The little five-year-old boy he'd lost in the spring certainly wasn't the first patient who had died on Grey. He wasn't even the first who shouldn't have died. By the time Grey found him, the child had already been weak from malnutrition and abuse. The diabetic condition had been known but never treated. Grey had fought to bring him out of the coma, and maybe he could have—if the little boy had an ounce of will to live.

A five-year-old baby who just didn't care.

Or a doctor who hadn't cared enough?

He couldn't sleep without the child's eyes haunting him. He was too aware of how exhausted he'd been that night. No one had forced him into volunteering the extra night hours in the south side clinic. His partnership practice on Chicago's north shore was busy enough. The long hours had caught up with him. He was tired of fighting battles that couldn't be won. He was tired of life, he was damned tired of death, and he'd brought that soul-deep exhaustion to the bedside of one small boy.

Guilt had eaten at him like a poison ever since. There was no antidote for the poison, because there was no way he could ever be absolutely sure that his failure as a doctor—and a man—could have affected the child's life. The issue had become immutable for Grey, as basic as air, time, wind. A doctor who lost his objectivity had no business practicing medicine. It was as simple as that.

Maybe you can be a carpenter, a voice inside him said. There's nothing wrong with being a carpenter. There would be something criminally wrong if you made a mistake with a patient because your judgment and objectivity are worth buckshot. Fifty yards away,

Jill disappeared inside the cabin. Root bent over the other man and rolled up the denim of the overalls on his left leg. The man's leg was heavy and muscular. It was also swollen at the knee. No cuts or abrasions, just swelling. The porch was too shadowed to see more, except that the man's boot sole was flopping. Jill didn't seem to have any neighbors who could afford shoes—or deodorant. He could practically smell the man from here. He's not your problem, he reminded himself. Jill returned to the porch, carrying a huge bowl in one hand and an armful of flowers in the other. Marigolds, one of the few species of flowers he could identify beyond roses.

Marigolds? Good Lord.

He squeezed his eyes closed and then awkwardly, determinedly pushed against the tree trunk to give him balance. As soon as he stood up, Wolf went into her teeth-baring, fur-raising act. Grey ignored her. Moisture bubbled on his forehead as he searched the ground for some kind of stick. He found a branch too tall to make much of a crutch, but it would do.

Stupid fever. He had to wait a few seconds for the dizziness to pass, and then he ambled, hobbling slow, toward the cabin. The dog's ears flattened. She snarled, blocking his path, but she backed up as Grey moved forward.

The two men glanced up at him as he approached but Jill never looked up. "Howdy there," Root greeted him. The old man's eyes were as shrewd as a boardroom president's. "Nice day."

"Hot."

"Wind's in the west. Fish always bite best when wind's in the west."

The old man passed on another half dozen sage remarks designed to keep a conversation about the weather going. Grey leaned against the porch pole and mentally exercised every four-letter word he knew. Fifty short yards and he felt whipped, battered and drained. He could also see what he hadn't been able to see from the distance.

The knee wasn't severely swollen. There was maybe a slight sprain, nothing more. The man's face was white, but his skin wasn't clammy. His eyes were clear—no signs of shock. Sweat rolled off his forehead, but that was half the heat and half the man's bulk. He'd bumped his knee, that was all that was wrong. You weren't going to treat him anyway, Treveran, Grey thought.

He felt the ironic pulse of relief in his heart, though, which irritated him. It hadn't come down to having to make a choice, for which he was grateful. Not just because of principles and honor. From the smell of the good ole boy, he hadn't had a bath in seven years.

That wasn't the only smell that wafted toward Grey. Jill had vinegar in the bowl and was stirring marigold petals into it with a wooden spoon. Grey would have raised his eyes to the sky in disgust, if the spending of any emotion didn't take so much energy. He straightened his good leg and let his body shift down to where he could sit and lean against the porch pole. Root was still talking to him. Wolf cradled close and applied a wet tongue to his face. He batted her away.

When Jill draped the marigold-vinegar compress on the man's knee, Grey's stomach developed an instant ulcer and his fingers itched.

"I know it's broke," whined the heavy-set man.

"It isn't broken. It'll be fine. When you get home, pack it in ice—"

"I ain't got no ice."

"Then cold cloths, well-water cold. And I'll give you some of this to use as a compress. Twenty minutes on, twenty minutes off. And stay off the leg for a couple of days."

"Told yer she wouldn't tell you to go to no doctor," Root told the man.

Jill's head lifted, green eyes leveled furiously on Root. "If it were a serious sprain, he'd belong at a doctor's. I've told you a hundred times, Root, I don't know anything more than a little first aid."

"Sure now, sure now," Root soothed her, but the look he passed to the other man was an explicit denial. "You go to some doctor, he wouldn't know about marigolds, now. She's got magic, just like her gran did."

"Root."

"I brought you a nice mess of fish for dinner," he said to divert her.

They all stayed an hour. Root filleted her fish; the injured man, called Hiram, rested with his leg up and Jill flew back and forth to the kitchen. She served water to the men, collected a bag of marigolds for Hiram to take home, and replaced the flesh-warmed compresses with new cold ones from time to time. The two men finally left, leaving the porch in total silence except for Wolf's wanton moans. Grey was scratching her ears.

Jill was aware of Grey. They'd been thrown together for the last four days and nights, and she was fast coming to the conclusion that it was impossible to be unaware of Grey. At the moment he was weak as a kitten, fast drawing conclusions about her neighbors, and apparently working mentally very hard to make some lethally serious judgments about her. Every time she moved, she felt the steady pulse of his cool black eyes on her. Impatience and frustration were better for him than apathy so she let him think what he liked.

Jill felt rueful. Sooner or later Grey was going to discover that the dog was always a sissy. Wolf's power as a baby-sitter and caretaker had just dissolved in the wind. And yes, Grey was looking at Jill with an expression that hinted at a slight inclination to get his hands around her neck.

"Marigolds, Jill?"

The towels and cloths and bowl were still cluttering the porch. She bent down to start cleaning up. "People around here are a little superstitious."

"I noticed."

She straightened. "No patience for superstitions, Treveran?"

"None."

"And you thought the marigolds were silly," she mused.

"I believe in magic just about as much as you do. You told him to use cold compresses and keep off the leg. That's what's going to make the knee feel better, not flowers. Which you knew."

"You're very sure of that?"

"Dead sure."

She smiled, pausing with her armload of cleanup at the door. "Marigolds," she said softly, "were one of the most common herbs used in the front-line hospitals during World War One. When the British ran short of medical supplies, they took to the fields. Internally, calendula herbs were used as a homeopathic arnica to treat for shock. Mixed with vinegar, they were used to bring down swelling."

He stared at her.

She tossed him her most whimsical smile. "Marigolds aren't magic, Treveran," she said firmly, "but after dinner I might be able to give you a taste of what is. You and I are going to make a little syrup of violets. A love potion. Then we'll see what you think."

The screen door banged behind her. Grey leaned back, closed his eyes and thought, My God. I'm holed up in this wilderness with a mad woman.

And her shorts weren't decent, either.

Three

Pansies and violets come from the same family. They've both been used in love potions since the beginning of time. You must have read *A Midsummer Night's Dream* when you were a kid. 'The juice of it on sleeping eyelids laid Will make a man or woman madly dote Upon the next live creature that it sees.' ''

She glanced at Grey. He was too preoccupied with shredding violet petals to respond. She turned away so he wouldn't see her grin. She measured twenty ounces of rectified spirits—vodka—and added it to the pot that already held thirty-five ounces of refined sugar.

Rain had been falling since sunset. It wasn't a horrendous storm, just a steady, cooling, life-giving mist. Wolf was outside moaning. She hated rain, but Jill didn't. Nothing soothed like soft lamplight and a cleansing rain after a long, tiring workday.

Grey was almost formally dressed—at least, he'd added a towel over his shoulders in lieu of a shirt. Until Root towed in his houseboat, she simply had no way to clothe him. The shirt she'd found Grey in had been shredded. Grey didn't seem to care about his clothes or his boat, except that the latter was obviously going to give him the means to leave her.

All through dinner she'd thought about whether she could let him go. He was in a hurry to be out of her way, and he was basically capable of climbing into a houseboat. But what about fixing food or maneuvering around on that swollen ankle? His fever kept coming and going, and fevers and water were a dangerous combination. Left alone, Grey was inclined to withdraw into a cobweb of sadness. And that was what seriously troubled Jill.

Of course, she couldn't force him to stay, but distracting Grey from whatever devils were haunting him, she'd discovered over dinner, wasn't at all hard.

"Alone, blue violets are a marvelous protection against wicked spirits," she continued lightly. "Together with lavender, they arouse lust and are one of the most powerful love stimulants there is. In fact—"

"Jill, would you quit talking nonsense and tell me how many more of these idiotic things you need."

Ignoring the last-straw patience in his voice, she peeked at his trayful. "A little more. You're not too fast with your hands, are you?"

"It's been a while since I've had practice plucking flowers. The only—*only*—reason I'm doing this is because I owe you."

"I really appreciate the help," she said gravely.

"No, you don't. The only reason you started this..." He stopped and glared at her. "I don't know why you started it. You could spend the next four years talking and you'd never convince me you believe in this."

"So cynical." She tch-tched, relieved him of the tray, stirred the petals in her syrup mixture and returned the tray to him so he could refill it. At that particular moment, she would have sold her soul for a camera. From his bushy brows to the shoulders that sprawled over the sides of the rocker to his hairy legs, Gray looked like a capital-M man. Surrounded by violets, though, he touched her sense of humor. His fingertips were already blue. He smelled wonderful. A petal was clinging to his chest; some had floated on his jeans. He kept brushing the flowers away like he was afraid they'd sting him.

"I'll tell you what cynical is. Wasting good vodka on some crazy violet juice."

"Syrup," she corrected.

"Whatever. You can't need more."

"I do. Did I tell you that another name for wild pansies was heart's ease? When you think about it, that name is much more fitting—"

"How about if we continue this conversation on a need-to-know basis."

"You're so sure you don't think you need to know any more about love potions? Their effects. How they work, what they—"

"Jill."

"Hmm?"

"I've been around you for four days. It's too late to convince me you're an idiot. I have no idea what, how or why you've got your backwoods friends thinking you're into hocus-pocus, but I've watched you brush your teeth. You do it just like I do." He lurched out of the rocker and hobbled over to her with the second filled tray of violet petals. "You want these thrown in there?"

"Please."

He dumped them, glared at the violet dye on his hands and sighed. He hobbled over to the water pump, picked up the cake of soap on the ledge, smelled it and sighed again. He leaned over and started lathering. "If you weren't a sane, intelligent fully grown woman, I would be inclined to worry about you."

"Heavens, why?" The syrup was bubbling gently, but it would take another hour or two before it boiled down and she could strain it.

Grey rinsed, splashed water on his face and neck and used a towel to haphazardly dry himself. His chest was still damp when he dropped to the bench seat at the table, stretched out his legs and leveled his hands on his knees. He cleared his throat. "I think it's time we had a little talk about hocus-pocus."

The expression in his eyes was bludgeon-black serious. "Sure," Jill said.

"You're a good lady."

"Thank you." He was struggling terribly for tact; she was trying not to grin.

"I figured out what you're doing here."

"I already told you what I was doing here," she said reproachfully.

He ignored that tone like he'd ignore an ant at a picnic. Jill wasn't incapable of being serious, but it was all uphill work getting her there. "I'm not talking about your soaps. I'm talking about what you're doing with your neighbors. They're people caught in a time warp, trying to make a living the way they did a hundred years ago on unforgiving land. No decent roads, no industry, no reason to draw them into the twentieth century. So you've got illiteracy and you've got less than ideal living conditions and you've got some superstitious, archaic ideas about health care."

"You've drawn a lot of conclusions from watching a few people visit my back door," Jill mentioned.

"Am I wrong?"

She hesitated. "No." She thought it was like Grey to sum up his observations in black and white.

"So you've got a pocket of poverty that's somehow escaped every federal and state agency that would have jumped in with food stamps and welfare."

"Welfare's valued on a level with spit in these parts," Jill mentioned. "Just because people are poor doesn't mean they aren't proud, that they don't have values that aren't important to them."

"If you're smart enough to figure that out, you're smart enough to figure out that they aren't your problem. Because that's what's happened, isn't it? Jill Stanton got caught in the middle when she plunked down here.''

"Heavens, one of us has been doing a dreadful amount of serious thinking," she said regretfully.

He enunciated carefully, in the vain hope it might make her listen. "I saw the girl who came to your door this morning. You gave her a pile of smelly leaves. You also gave her some good sound counseling about sanitation, washing herself up, clean health habits. And the good old boy this afternoon—you showered him with good advice before you draped him with flowers," he added mildly. "I've noticed Jill Stanton has a real problem turning people away. She takes in basket cases from a storm, for example."

Jill frowned. "Honestly, you've really been a lot more trouble than a simple basket case—"

He raised his voice. "Only what I can't figure out is why she doesn't just sell the common sense without the hocus-pocus."

"I don't *sell* anything to the people around here."

"Let's not split straws."

"What if I told you I believed in magic?"

"I would politely suggest that you were full of horseflies."

Her gaze narrowed on Grey briefly. Then she straightened from her crouched position on the hearth and walked to the cupboard. She poured a glass from a brown jug and handed it to Grey. "It's just wine, and homemade as you might have expected. I would have offered it to you before, but I thought you would mind.''

He took a long sip and admitted it was delicious. ''You thought I would mind it was homemade?''

''No,'' she said blithely. ''I thought you would mind that it was violet wine. I already told you that anything with violets has love-potion properties. And not just love, but the ability to make you see things differently, affect your attitude toward love and life.''

''Jill?''

''Hmm?''

''I want you to watch how worried I am.'' He finished the glass in three gulps.

She smiled.

That smile gnawed at him long after they'd both gone to bed. He lay in the dark and listened to the rain. His ankle throbbed, but that wasn't why he couldn't sleep.

He'd never met a person who didn't have quirks. He certainly had his share. He always slept on the right side of the bed, had a habit of putting his left shoe on first, and—although he'd never admit it—he never raised an umbrella inside a building. To judge someone else had never been Grey's way. To each their own. The most brilliant people had their superstitions; the most practical always had an impractical side. People were interesting exactly because of that tendency to be unpredictable.

Only the confounded woman went too far. Love potions. Syrup of violets. Chamomile and marigolds and ox-eyed daisies. Jill *refused* to be logical.

And he couldn't get the damn woman off his mind.

The bedsprings creaked every time he shifted positions. The pillow was too hot, too soft. He bunched it up one way, then another. If he were in Chicago, he could have slept. He needed some nice loud traffic sounds, a few sirens, a few screeched brakes. The whole problem with the countryside was that it was too quiet. A good rain in Chicago would have pattered and splattered and made a predictable racket on the windows. Here, the rain drifted down in a hush and it smelled like violets. The whole damn world smelled like violets.

"Can't sleep?"

Grey turned his head the instant he heard Jill's voice in the doorway. "I'm fine."

"Turn on your stomach. I'll give you a rubdown."

"No, I'm fine. Go back to sleep."

She disappeared—he hoped permanently—but she returned within minutes carrying something. The night was too dark to identify more than shadows, but he could see she was wearing something short and white. Too short. Too white. It was altogether easier when he didn't have to think of her as a woman and could just think of her as a demented caretaker set on this earth to personally drive him bananas.

"Can you turn over comfortably with that ankle or do you want some help?" she asked peaceably.

"Go back to sleep, Jill."

"Crabbiness is always a good sign of healing, and forced inactivity without exercise is the same as asking for insomnia. You're probably sore all over, achy." She yawned sleepily. "So...you can roll over on your stomach nice and polite, or you can make a big fuss and I'll have to get tough. Your choice."

"You have a hearing problem. Go back in your own room. Please."

She yawned again, but she didn't move.

In time, frustratingly aware that she wasn't going to leave until he complied, he heaved over on his stomach. Fast and smooth, she skimmed the sheet down to his waist and climbed on the bed next to him. He heard her rubbing her hands together and then felt a warm, thick oil layering on his back. Not surprising him at all, it smelled like spice and flowers. When and if he escaped this woman, his entire body was going to require fumigation before he rejoined civilization.

"Do you tense when anyone touches you or is it just me? Loosen up, dearie dumps."

In spite of himself, he could feel a smile forming in the darkness. "I don't suppose it would help if I mentioned one more time that I don't want a rubdown?"

"Don't be a goose. There isn't a body on this earth of any age who doesn't love a back rub. Even crabby cases like you, Treveran."

What was he supposed to say? He mumbled irritably, "I just don't want you thinking you have to do things like this."

"You would worry about something like that," she murmured. "Silly man, I'm not doing this for you,

I'm doing it for me. This is just another terrific excuse to get my hands on your body. One look at your vertebrae and I have a lust attack. And your shoulder blades! My knees get all quivery just thinking about your shoulder bla—'' Her hands stilled. ''Good heavens. Was that a chuckle I heard? Laughter? Coming from old sad eyes?''

''Shut up, will you, Jill?''

''Hmm.''

There were back rubs and there were back rubs. Some were a natural part of love play between a man and a woman. Then there were the kind that Jill gave. She showed no mercy. She took a tight muscle as a personal affront. She viewed flesh as personal prey. No ache was sacred. She used whatever worked—the heel of her hands and her fists and her fingers. Whatever turned a man into raving, helpless putty.

That he was capable of relaxing startled Grey. He hadn't felt the stress flow out of his body in weeks, maybe months. It startled him even more when he became aroused. He could have sworn he was dead inside, not just to the touch of a woman but to feelings, any feelings.

The heels of her hands kneaded the small of his back. ''You love that, don't you, sexy?'' she murmured.

When she was through pummeling his back into jelly, her fingers soothed and smoothed and softened. Unyielding flesh became resilient. Ingrained aches dissolved. A man who had no tolerance, belief or patience in the whimsical began to believe in spells.

Jill was all shadows, all scents, all tease. That's what she'd been since he'd met her. The illusions were getting worse instead of better.

At last she stopped. "You'll sleep now," she whispered with utter confidence.

One instant she had her bare foot on the floor and was climbing off the bed. The next she was lying flat, next to him on the mattress. She was too shocked to feel any other reaction but surprise.

So was Grey. He didn't think he had the strength to reach for Jill and he certainly never intended to. It just happened. The instinct was less desire than despair. He was beginning to think that his sanity hovered on the brink of scents, sounds, textures and touch, all of which linked to Jill. That wasn't rational.

She was only a woman.

But maybe he just had to be sure of that. His palm cradled her head and his mouth lowered on hers. Her breath was no more than a wisp of wind and for a moment her eyes were open. Her lashes shuttered down when his lips molded over hers. He felt her fingertips fluttering on his arms, climbing with tentative sureness to his neck. She arched her throat to meet the pressure of his mouth. She tasted like surprise, like freshness, like wonder. She kissed like she wanted to share those things.

He kissed her again and again. He knew it was never going to go too far because he hadn't the strength, the energy. He was also positive he didn't have desire. This was just . . . need. The need to feel the texture of her skin, to tangle his fingers in her hair, to reduce fantasy and imagination to simpler mediums. The bleat of pulse in her throat was just a woman's pulse. The small breast swelling through thin cloth against his chest was just a woman's breast. The lips yielding, pliant and supple beneath his, were just a woman's lips.

She was just Jill.

The ache exploding inside him was madness. Not desire.

Jill was swept up in far sweeter emotions. The room was so dark. He tasted of such loneliness, such desperation. His hands groped over her like a lost man seeking something to hold on to. The sheet tangled between them, and the rain kept falling in hushed silence.

As soft as a secret, desire whispered through her. Combined with the warmth and empathy she felt, it was far more compelling than anything she'd ever known. Grey's need called to something private and feminine and powerful inside her—the need to give. The need to touch, share, heal.

So careful of his cuts and bruises, she let her hands play light music over his skin. Aware that the brace on his ankle made his movement difficult, she was the one who surged closer. Never forgetting the swollen sore on his temple, she let her lips roam over his face and throat, dropping kisses of comfort, promises, tenderness. Simple caring didn't have to be complicated, but he didn't seem to know that.

Maybe she'd forgotten how good it felt to hold a man. Maybe that was also why everything suddenly changed. A woman could drown in a hush of rain, a black night, the liquid sensation of flesh on flesh. Thinking of Grey, what he wanted, what he needed, was so easy. The sudden roaring in her ears was not.

She wasn't sure when Grey's kisses changed. At first there was no aggression, no force. Then, maybe, the lost man had finally discovered feeling and remembered that he was once a lover. Lips that explored suddenly claimed. The palm sweeping over breast and thigh turned intimate, possessive. A thumb discovered that a small nubbin of a nipple could be incomparably sensitive. That thumb cherished, coaxed, deliberately aroused a deeper response.

Cool sheets had turned hot. Her nightgown had skimmed up to her waist. In a second's flash, dread pulsed through Jill on a violent wave of nausea.

A shudder, like icy fingers were shaking her, took over her body. Heart pounding, blind with horror, she lurched up and away—away from skin, away from heat, away from contact.

"Jill? Honey, what—"

She tried to sound light, brisk, normal. "I can't imagine what the two of us were thinking of. You have to sleep. You're hurt; for heavens' sakes, you still have a fever—"

His fingers closed on her wrist. "How did I hurt you? What happened, Jill?"

"Nothing. *Nothing.*" The catch in her throat was huge and thick. His impossibly gentle tenor only made it worse. She pushed at his hand, freeing herself from his grasp. She wasn't sure what she was afraid of, only knew that she was drowning in it. "Go to sleep, Grey. Leave me alone. Please."

She escaped his room and flew past hers. The living room was still, silent, dark. Everything in the room was as familiar as her childhood—the smell of wood ash in the hearth, the hand carved desk, the old sofa with a creaking spring. She huddled in the giant cushioned rocker that belonged to Gran, knees drawn up, arms wrapped around them. She couldn't have been shaking harder if she'd been hurled naked in snow.

She closed her eyes tight, but that didn't stop stark, raw pictures from flashing in her head. Ugly pictures. A man's fist slamming toward her face. The shattering of a mirror, a scream. And herself, huddled in a corner, vulnerable and helpless, arms around her head, waiting for another blow to land, no longer crying, too terrified to cry.

The voice in her mind was as vicious as a rage. *Put it out of your mind, damn it.*

But she thought she had.

She was sure she had.

Salt stung behind her closed eyelids. Confused and shaky, she pushed at her hair with sweat-dampened fingers. The night when Michael had broken in her apartment had nothing to do with Grey. Fear that Grey would hurt her hadn't existed, not when she'd been all but bare in bed with him, and not now.

Why she'd panicked made no sense. She was a grown woman entitled to feel desire, want, need. She'd felt a bond with Grey from the beginning. Maybe it wasn't love and maybe it was mixed up with compassion and saving his life and empathy. What did the labels matter? She cared. The last she knew, caring was a clean, strong, good emotion and touching him—Lord!—Grey had so much passion in him. The surge of want, the delicious sensation of weakness, the excitement of yearning had swept over her like a surprise, unique to what she could ever remember feeling with any man.

So what happened, Jill? she asked herself silently.

I don't know, I don't know...

There had just been one instant, one flavor, one taste...of being terrifyingly vulnerable. Not just physically vulnerable, like with Michael, but something much more powerful and threatening. Grey had made her feel vulnerable from the soul, but what should have been special and wonderful simply was not. The sensation of helplessness had been unbearable, intolerable, awesome and awful.

She could still feel it.

Wolf sneaked in on fur-padded paws. She sat down and methodically, patiently, thoroughly started to wash Jill's bare toes. Any other time Jill would have laughed.

Not tonight.

It wasn't easy to tiptoe around with a broken ankle. When it came down to it, Grey hadn't been much of a tiptoer before the broken ankle. He couldn't use the cane because it made too much noise on the wooden floor, and hopping made a thumping racket. Traveling had never seemed so complex. All he wanted to do was silently get past her door and into the kitchen.

By the time he made it, he felt as smug as a cat with a canary. His ankle was throbbing like hell, but he hadn't wakened her.

The windows announced a pearl-pale sunrise. The room was still invaded with the smell of violets, and a dozen vials and bottles stood on the table next to her syrup brew from the night before. He knew where she kept the wine and he knew where she kept the plates. He had no idea where she'd keep a tray.

There was a wicker basket thing on the hearth with some kind of roots mounded in it. By the time he discarded the roots and carried the basket to her dry sink, he had to wait for the draining weakness to pass.

Nuts, raisins and fruit. That's what she liked for breakfast, which made it easy enough. She kept the nuts below the dry sink, and raisins in sealed bags in the hutch by the table. He filled two bowls and carried a third empty one to the door. She kept fresh fruit in the well pit, fifteen yards from the kitchen door. As soon as his head stopped spinning, he'd be headed there. Jill got up with the sun. He couldn't dawdle.

He heaved an annoyed sigh, heard only by the birds, and started out. Walt Disney should film such adventures. The porch had three steps; the well pit had six. Her lawn wouldn't qualify for a golf course. The grasses were knee tall, sticky with dew, and the walking cane she'd fixed him sank into the damp ground. Mosquitoes were up as early as the birds. He couldn't

swat them, use the cane and carry the bowl of strawberries, too.

By the time he was back in the kitchen and had
everything arranged on the tray, he stopped to rest
again. If he'd slept the night before, he was positive
that the fever would now be gone and that he wouldn't
still be this weak. As it happened, he hadn't slept at
all, and he had no time to sleep now.

Balancing the tray one-handed, he and the cane
hobbled toward her bedroom. He rapped once on her
half-open door and then entered.

He hadn't been in her room before, but it suited her.
The bedstead was old brass and big; the bed was more
pillows than Jill, and the feather mattress was covered with a patchwork quilt in wild colors. Plants
clustered under the windows and books piled on books
against one wall. She'd refinished an old steamer
trunk. Its leather gleamed, its brass shone. The draw-
ers in the ancient wardrobe were half open. Jill wasn't
neat. Pinks and greens and yellows spilled out, bras,
tops, pants. Her chief criterion for clothes was obviously color. A square mirrored dish held approxi-
mately nine thousand pairs of earrings.

As white witches went, his had a definite flamboy-
ant spirit. Grey had always thought he could give or
take flamboyance as a personality trait until last night,
when Jill had lost hers.

Exactly how, when, where or why he'd managed to
hurt her, he didn't know. It also didn't matter. He had.

He cleared his throat. The bundle on the bed didn't
move. He cleared his throat again, and like a haywire

spring she suddenly bolted to a sitting position, panic
in her eyes and alarm in her expression. Sun poured in
the window, kissing her face. The white nightgown
was half slipped off her bare shoulder. He saw the
vulnerability in her face, he saw her bare shoulder and
he saw the heavy violet shadows under her eyes.

He lowered his gaze. "Thought you'd like breakfast," he said heartily. Maybe she didn't, but she was
getting it. There wasn't a chance in hell he could balance the tray for another thirty seconds. The three
bowls skidded to the edge of the basket when he set it
on the bed.

"Looks like it's going to be another swelterer. I
don't understand this country. It's either a hundred
and ten or it's raining." He fumbled awkwardly with
the cover around her waist, trying to smooth it out to
make some kind of table. It wouldn't flatten. Jill
didn't have any flat edges. "Nuts," he announced
briskly. "I noticed before that you love nuts." He in-
jected more enthusiasm in his voice. "I *know* you like
raisins." Both bowls threatened to tip. His whole body
was threatening to tip. "And strawberries..."

Three spilled, one on the floor. There wasn't any
way he could pick up the one on the floor. Maybe she
hadn't noticed they'd fallen. Where was the damn dog
when he needed it?

"Well," he said cheerfully, "you have breakfast.
Relax. I never intended to get in your way. I was just
headed for my room."

He made it to the door before her voice sliced
through the silence. "If you're going to be this nice to

me all day, I'm going to shuttle you off to a sanitarium for serious treatment." Her blithe tone dropped like a bucket. "Grey, I owe you an explanation. And an apology."

For seventy-two hours he'd been trying to get a serious word out of her. She was serious now and he wished she weren't. She'd cried the night before. It was in her eyes, and so was an honesty that tore at him. "You'll never owe me a damn thing, Jill. I'm the one in debt."

He made it to his room before the sweat broke out on his forehead. The cane slipped from his fingers as he sagged on the bed. His jeans were dew damp at the bottom of the leg; he didn't care.

He had to do better than breakfast in bed but that was all he could manage for now. In fact, he didn't think he could manage anything at this particular given moment. Stars swarmed under his closed eyelids. Heat swamped him, and then darkness.

Four

He was obviously going to pretend that last night had never happened. Jill reached into her clothes basket for a pair of pants, took two clothespins out of her mouth and hung the pants up by the legs. Through the inverted V she could see Grey.

When he'd awakened an hour before, she'd ordered him to the hammock with a *Wall Street Journal*. Possibly he wasn't overly interested in week-old *Wall Street Journal*s, because every time she looked up he threw a smile in her direction. For four days she'd been trying to win smiles out of him, but not smiles like that. Not soothing, reassuring, relax-Jill-I'll-never-touch-you-again-as-long-as-you-live smiles.

She leaned over for another item in the clothes basket, and came up with his jeans. Grey was wearing a towel. If Root didn't tow her visitor's houseboat soon, a towel was going to become his permanent attire. His jeans hadn't been much more than ragbag material before she'd washed them.

He hadn't said a word when she'd confiscated his jeans, and he'd sat as still as a passive cupcake when she'd told him she was going to apply mallow compresses on his stubborn-to-heal wasp stings. Whenever he wasn't smiling, he was drinking the black willow tea next to him.

Such marvelous obedience. Such a total change in personality. She was tempted to walk over there and hit him.

Jill jammed another three clothespins in her mouth and reached for another item of clothing. He was treating her like precious, priceless crystal. She was not precious; she was not priceless. She was just a woman with a few nasty memories—memories that she'd thought she'd completely obliterated from her life—and a stupid, idiotic feeling of fragility that had haunted her all day.

She was strong enough to handle what had happened to her with her ex-husband, and strong enough to be honest about it.

And if Grey said one more word to her in that tender, gentle tenor, she was probably going to burst into tears.

I seem to be slightly confused this afternoon, she thought. Slightly? She couldn't have been more relieved when she noticed two shadows moving in the woods. Her visitors turned into Billy and Faith Winters.

Billy was fourteen, and of that adolescent age when his long limbs and big feet constantly got in his way. He escaped farm work and his father whenever he could to visit her, not because he didn't like farm work and his father, but because he had an exhaustively painful crush on her. As the two neared, his face grew red from the simple act of looking at her. His color was not unnoticed by his mother, who greeted Jill with a deadpan wink.

Faith's face was like a weathered avocado, worn and sun-leathered and heavy around the jaws. If she was barely forty, she looked twenty years older. She wore a man's work boots and a faded calico dress. She'd delivered each of her nine children alone and the fortitude and strength that were part of her character showed in her gait, her face, her friendly smile.

"I'll help you finish that, Jill." On the other side of the line, she reached for a blouse and a clothespin.

"I've got tea in the house."

"Don't need a thing. Just visited Sue Ellen. That baby of hers is due in another month. I swear she's big as a barn."

Jill didn't happen to know Sue Ellen or any of the other people that Faith casually gossiped about for the next few minutes. She waited patiently, already knowing the reason for her neighbor's visit. Billy had all too deliberately ambled over to Grey, obviously to garner his attention. She could have told them both that Grey was more than capable of listening to Faith and handling Billy at the same time.

"How's the family?" she prodded Faith gently.

"Fine, fine. Except my youngest, of course." Faith pursed her lips. "That's kind of why I came to see you. For Tommy."

Jill nodded gently. "I've been thinking about him since you brought him over."

"The other eight, they're all fine. Never been a bit of problem to me. But Tommy, he's been teched from the day he was born. Sweet boy. He just ain't right." Faith's hopeless eyes glinted with desperation at Jill. "My grandmother used to do something with the primroses. I thought you might know. They're up in my garden, but I don't know what to do with them. I'd sure pay you. I'd pay yer anything I had."

"No need for that. And there are primroses coming up wild in the field; I'll fix you up something right here." It didn't take long to collect primrose petals and a handful of seeds from a black mustard plant. Grey was out of hearing range when she went off with Faith, but they walked right past him on the way to the porch. Jill brought a glass of cool well water while the older woman mopped her brow.

"I'll sew it up in his pillow tonight. It's just what I was hoping fer, Jill. It'll help him; I know it will."

"I hope so, too," Jill murmured, and not a soul could have told she was less than a serious believer of the faith cure. "It could be that we need something stronger than that, though, Faith."

"Ain't nothing stronger, my grandmother always tole me. Used to be a man in the far woods, madder than a hoot owl. It was the primrose spell that calmed him just fine."

"Yes," Jill agreed, "but your Tommy isn't mad like that. He's just a little different."

"Teched," his mother admitted.

"I had a dream about him the other night. A powerful dream." She had to turn so her face was averted from Grey's vision. He distracted her, and for more reasons than what had happened between them last night. Faith was worth more than distraction, and so was her retarded four-year-old little boy. "I dreamed Tommy was better, much better, but that what it took to make him better was a trip. I saw the place in my dreams—a brick building, a lot of grass and trees—"

Faith said haughtily, "I ain't taking my boy to no government place. I ain't takin' him nowhere. He belongs with me and his pa. He'd pine without us somethin' fierce. I won't do that to him." Then she hesitated. "But there now. I didn't mean to interrupt your dream."

Jill said soothingly, "In that dream he wasn't alone. He was holding my hand. The place had lots of windows, lots of sunshine. There were lots of other little boys like Tommy and he loved it. You know, Faith, I know a place just like that, and I would be glad to take him there—"

"I don't think so..." Faith started firmly, and then stopped. "My grandmother always put a lot of store in dreams."

"So did mine."

"Terrible upsetting, some dreams."

"I know. My best guess is that I'll have that same dream about Tommy again. I'll sure tell you if I do." Jill added, "Of course it won't ever have to come to that if the primroses work. You see if they make a difference in Tommy. If they don't, then come back and we'll talk again."

Faith and Billy both collected a hug before they left. Jill waited several minutes before wandering over to Grey. In contrast to before, he wasn't alternately sipping tea or smiling at her. His face was buried in the *Wall Street Journal*.

"Your jeans shouldn't take more than another half an hour to dry," she told him.

"Fine." The newspaper tip fluttered in the breeze, but it never showed his face.

"If you're going to say something, let's have it. Don't tell me you weren't listening."

"I heard every word," Grey agreed mildly.

"I can imagine exactly what you were thinking when I handed her the primrose and black mustard spell."

"Can you?" Grey finally peeled down his paper and leveled his eyes on Jill. "I was thinking that you were quite a witch, Jill. You keep exercising those powers, and you just might talk that woman into getting the boy in a special school in time."

For the first time since last night, he saw the tension leave her face. Sparkle popped back in her eyes and mischief flavored her grin. "Maybe there's hope

for you, Treveran. By next week I might even have you
believing in love potions.''
   ''Jill?''
   ''Hmm?''
   ''Don't hold your breath.''

The bracken fire was burning low. Dinner had been
rabbit steaks cooked on sticks over the fire, bowls of
sweet red berries and some kind of baked root that had
tasted like yams. Grey had taken care not to ask in case
they weren't.

For the first time in days he'd had an appetite. Sated
now, he watched a fire-red sun lower to the creek ho-
rizon. The splash of water was the only sound in the
still woods. Wolf's head occasionally bobbed up, then
Jill's. Both had sleek wet heads and a violent love for
the water. The game of fetch the stick alternated with
a game of race. Neither was serious about either.

The creek dropped off to deep water at the end of
the dock. Green waters gradually turned black as the
sun set. The woods took on a stillness, a peace. The
bracken fire still released a sweet smell, an occasional
puff of smoke. Grey added another handful of ferns—
not because he really believed they warded off mosquitoes, like Jill said, but because he needed something to do.

A man with nothing to do on a hot night might be
slightly inclined to obsession with the naked woman in
the water. It had been her suggestion to cook dinner by
the creek, and his for her to indulge in a swim. She'd
hesitated about the swim—she had no suit with her.

And she'd given in to the suggestion, he guessed, for exactly the same reason. Jill, being Jill, would have taken skinny-dipping as a natural choice if he hadn't been there, and her eyes had been a marvelous defiant green as she'd peeled off her top and shorts an hour ago. *See, Grey? It's nothing. A body's a body's a body. I've seen yours and it's certainly no big deal if you see mine. Nothing's changed since last night.*

Everything, of course, had changed since last night.

He popped a last stick on the fire and leaned forward, legs spread, massaging the knee above the cast. If he'd been alone, he would have brooded about his own problems. Being anywhere near Jill made it impossible to think about his own problems. Half the time she made it impossible for him to think, period.

He still didn't understand what had happened the night before. He'd never expected her wild sweet responsiveness, and he had no explanation for how powerfully the wave of desire had swept over him. He still didn't know what he could have done or said to make her bolt like a wounded fawn. Maybe they were like chalk and cheese; maybe she was whimsical and a little crazy and occasionally irritating and volatile and even downright upsetting. But he would have broken his other ankle before deliberately hurting Jill.

Two wet forms hurled themselves out of the water and raced for the bushes just beyond their fire. He heard Jill swear—a rarity—and guessed that Wolf had tried to shake off a creek full of water on her. She was laughing, though. He saw her arms fly in the air when she pulled her T-shirt back on. It wasn't pitch black yet, though he could probably have located that T-shirt if it were. Chartreuse was the color. He also caught several glimpses of a bare white fanny. He had to remind himself how many hundreds of white fannies he'd seen in his day.

By the time she parted the branches to walk toward him, he considered mentioning to her that donning clothes over a soaking wet body was as sensible as leaving an umbrella home on a rainy day. Her hair was plastered to her head, wet-rat style. The T-shirt announced that Jill was inexorably female, and the blue shorts fit more snugly than underpants. Water was still streaming down her legs, her lips were blue and her skin was wrinkled.

Desire shot through him, an honest source of worry. Wanting a woman in that condition was not sane.

"That dog tried to kill me," she said.

"I saw. She also beat you in two out of three races."

"That's not fair. She didn't wait until I said go. Down, you beast. Go lay down until you're dry." Jill's finger sent the animal slinking off to the creek edge. Jill's face registered instant guilt.

Grey pushed two fingers at his temples, trying to smother a smile.

Arms crossed, she crouched by the fire. "The water was freezing."

"It didn't appear to inhibit the two of you. I was beginning to think you both had something genetically in common with a porpoise."

"It was Wolf's fault. She didn't want to get out."

"Ah."

She shook a stick at him. "That 'ah,' Treveran, reeks of condescending, know-it-all, sexist, masculine superiority."

"Probably. Now come on over here before you catch pneumonia."

"I beg your pardon?"

"The fire's no more than three coals and a spark at this point. You're not going to get warm there." He motioned to the spot between his straddled legs, where he was holding the blanket she'd brought as a tablecloth. Its texture was rough and one side was covered with dirt and leaves, but it would keep her from shivering. He would have brought it to her if it didn't take so much confounded effort to get up, walk and get back down again.

"I'll take it—"

"Just sit down," he said impatiently. So she chose a spot near his feet, which meant he had to awkwardly scoot forward to drape the blanket on her shoulders. He would also naturally have rubbed her blanketed back and arms to dry her if she hadn't instantly tensed up. Until last night, such basic contact would never have bothered Jill.

He hesitated and then backed off, dropping the triangle edge of blanket over her head like a hood. She peeled it up, and whipped him a grin that almost convinced him he'd imagined her reaction.

"The blanket over my head—are you trying to tell me that my hairstyle leaves something to be desired?"

"I said nothing, absolutely nothing."

"I forgot a comb," she said despairingly.

"Somehow that doesn't surprise me."

"Oh, shut up, Treveran." She sighed, rubbing the blanket absently at her damp locks. "Luckily it's just you and me. And impressing you with my fantastic beauty isn't on my list of priorities." She added seriously, "Your fever's been down since this afternoon."

He nodded. "I'll be out of your hair as soon as that neighbor of yours tows my boat."

Slowly she drew up her legs and wrapped the blanket close around her. Behind her, Grey leaned back and used an arm behind his head for a pillow.

"Whether or not you have a fever, you're a long way from being ready to cope alone, Grey," she said slowly.

"I may not be in shape to run races for a while, but I'll manage."

She hesitated. "So where would you take the boat once Root brings it in?"

"Nowhere. Anywhere. It doesn't much matter. It's rented for another month."

She hesitated again. "And then where will you go?"

His eyes never opened, and the words came out slow and a little clipped. "I don't know."

"You must have a job."

"I did. I don't now."

Absently she plucked a handful of grass at her side. "You were never married?" When he didn't respond, she probed cheerfully, "Your driver's license said you were thirty-four, and being as unequivocably handsome as you are, Treveran, there must be a woman in your life.''

"We seem to be,'' Grey said dryly, "a little nosy tonight.''

"Yes, we are.'' Her tone was blithe, but determined.

He took his time before saying anything else. "I never married, but for about seven years I was the same as. She couldn't have children, which was partly why she was shy of legal entanglements. We lived together. Now what else would you like to pry into?''

"Did you love her?''

"I loved her. Heart, soul, flowers, the whole bit. The relationship gradually faded into too much convenience and too little commitment—for both of us. That was about four years ago. Would you like a detailed list of the women I've had occasional relationships with since?''

"Yes.''

"Lay off, honey.'' The brood in his voice was flavored with ice. "Whether I have a job, whether I have a woman, where I go is not your problem. I've been handling my own life for thirty-four years. And I've intruded for far too many days on yours. Admit it. You'll be glad when I'm gone.''

Mentally she agreed. As soon as Grey left, she wouldn't have anyone who needed waiting on hand and foot. She wouldn't have to make special meals. She'd have more time to work on building up her business, and that wouldn't wait if she expected to bring in serious cash flow. And once Grey left, nothing like last night could ever happen again. Last night her life, which had seemed safe and sound and secure, had threatened to shatter in little pieces.

She stared at the fire's last embers. They looked like jewels, like orange diamonds. In the distance, a hoot owl announced he was serious about finding prey. Frogs noisily croaked their lonely desire for mates at the creek edge. The water flowed with a sound like silver, and a crescent moon peeked between the trees.

The woods were peaceful and still. At any other time but tonight, the smells of earth and green and growing things would make her think of life, of renewal and continuity and promise.

Everything Grey had said upset her. Damn it, he had no one. No place to go, no person to go to, and apparently no job to occupy his time. He was in as much shape to take care of himself as a newborn bear cub. When Root actually got around to towing Grey's boat was, of course, totally unknown. Root had said tomorrow, but he'd also said that the day before. Root ran on back hills time, which had no conceivable relationship to schedules or clocks or timetables. Soon, though, was inevitable.

Jill plucked another handful of grass. Secrets were pulling at her like shadows. "When I moved here," she said quietly, "I was at a pretty rough point in my life. Sometimes everyone needs a place, a little space and time and privacy. I think that's where you are now. I know it's where I was a few months ago."

His eyes opened when she turned to face him. Her hair had dried in wisps of silk and her face was white by moonlight.

"I'd been divorced for a year, but my ex-husband wouldn't let me alone," she continued. "When I married Michael, I could have sworn he was one of the kindest, gentlest men alive. He was a stranger by the time I left." She took a long breath. "He was an alcoholic, and I felt a lot of guilt about leaving him. It felt like kicking a man when he was down, like deserting ship, like flipping marriage vows out the window because the going got a little rough."

"Jill—" Grey interrupted.

She was trying to single-handedly destroy all the soft grasses growing in her touch zone. She was so cold, suddenly. Not creek-swimming cold but soul cold. She crossed her arms and determinedly kept talking. "I couldn't help him, Grey, and couldn't make him get help. Any feelings of love I had were dead, but that isn't why I left. I stayed as long as I could, but selfish or not, leaving him came down to survival. Literal survival. My ex-husband was quite positive that I was responsible for everything that had gone wrong in his life. Michael wouldn't have swatted a fly when he was sober, but when he had a few drinks under his belt..."

The pictures in Grey's head were making him sick, not because of what she said but because of all she was obviously leaving out. His instinct was to reach out and hold her, now, immediately. He didn't. She was sitting small and fragile, a crushable pride in the tilt of her chin, her shallow breathing measuring her desire for control. She didn't want to spill tears in front of a stranger.

He had to remind himself that that was all he was, a stranger passing through her life for a few days. But all he could think of was how easily he'd been fooled by her lazy velvet voice and a pair of river-deep eyes. Jill had been to hell and back. He'd been too insensitive, too wrapped up in his own problems, to see.

Jill suddenly jumped up and stretched, all brisk energy and feminine determination. "Time to get the walking wounded home—that's you, dearie dumps. And in case you're wondering, there was a reason I told you my soap opera." She grabbed the blanket and started folding it. "Actually there were two reasons. I just couldn't say nothing, letting you think I bolted last night because of something you did. What happened was my fault, not yours. Maybe an old nightmare caught up with me; I don't know and I don't care and I don't want to talk about it. Anyway—"

"Honey—"

"Treveran, I'm having an anxiety attack trying to get all this out; would you please not interrupt?" She colored her grin sassy, too aware that his intense dark eyes refused to leave her face. "I want to talk about you, handsome. You've been a lot of trouble, I'm not denying it. But I think if you'll zip off your pride you'll admit you're in no shape to take care of yourself yet. What I'm trying to tell you is that I've been in your shoes—hit a spot where I needed a place, a little breather, a little space from the madding crowd. I'm not asking you to stick around; I'm sure not going

to waste my breath coaxing you, but I think I'm...
daring you to stay."

"Daring?" He leaned up and reached for his stick,
a dozen thoughts in his head pulled up short by her
odd choice of words.

"Daring you to," she repeated. "I've been telling
you since you got here that there's magic in these
woods, Grey. Dangerous magic. The kind of magic
that makes you want to believe in sunshine when the
whole damn world's trying to crash all around you.
The kind of magic that will heal wounds no medicine
can possibly heal. You don't believe it? I do. And
maybe I'm suggesting that one of the reasons you're
in such a fast hurry to get away from here is that
you're afraid. Just a little afraid. Just a smidgeon.
That the magic might be real."

Daring Grey with magic was like expecting Cinder-
ella to fit in a size-ten triple-E shoe. Jill didn't expect
him to respond; she just wanted him to think about
staying.

Not looking at him, she swiftly brushed dirt over the
fire and gathered up the silverware. Telling him about
her ex-husband had drained and upset her. There had
seemed no other way to let him know that he was not
alone in having traveled some rough roads.

Guilt lanced through her when she watched Grey
start out walking. Her desire to heal his emotional
wounds had made it too easy to forget his physical
ones. His fever was finally gone, but this had been the
first long patch of hours he'd been up and around.
Exhaustion and strain were now tightening the lines on

his face, and the path was so dark and uneven that walking was difficult for him even with the cane. Of course, Grey would never ask for help, but when he stumbled once a lump filled her throat.

He stumbled a second time. She simply shifted the blanket to her other arm and firmly dropped an anchoring arm around his waist. With the contact, he stopped and looked at her—only for seconds.

Grey's eyes were dark and searching, and she was suddenly supremely conscious of the supple feel of his warm skin, the isolation of night and woods. She wanted him. She could feel it like a hum in her blood, like a lush welling in the most intimate corners of her soul. Sexuality was only part of it. She wanted the rights to share, give, grow, heal, know him in a way she knew no other man.

A shiver touched her in an echo of panicked vibrations she'd felt the night before. If a simple arm around his waist aroused this huge a feeling of vulnerability... but Jill quickly blocked the sensations. She also dropped her arm the very instant they reached the clearing to the cabin.

"You need anything before we turn in?" she asked him at the porch.

"Not a thing, Jill."

Relief was a sing in her smile. His voice was normal, easy, quiet. He didn't realize how much his touch affected her, and she didn't want him to.

All she wanted was a pillow and the nearest mattress. It had been a long and oddly upsetting day, and she'd been up most of the previous night. Alone in her bedroom, she barely found the energy to strip off clothes and don a nightshirt before diving for the covers.

She slept like the dead—for all of an hour. The groans she heard seemed half out of a dream. When she realized they were coming from Grey's room, she flew from her bed.

Night air chilled her skin as she groped through the hall. She heard another groan when she reached his doorway. "It's just me, Grey. What happened?" Moonlight had turned the room into the shadowed color of mushrooms. She could make out his face, ash-white on the pillows. "What's wrong? I thought you were doing so well..." Her palm swept his forehead. It felt cool.

"The ankle. It's driving me crazy. And my head. God, my head...."

Her stomach bunched with alarm. Grey never complained. He'd never once even admitted to pain before. He'd certainly never asked for her help. "Just stay still. I'll light a lamp and get you something—"

"No." His fingers closed over her wrist. His grip was strong, startling her. "Just stay with me for a little while, would you?"

"I could make you some—"

"No, I don't need anything. I just don't want to be alone for a few minutes."

Sleepily she guessed he was having nightmares again and was too proud to admit it. "No problem, I'll just pull up the rocker."

"You'll just be uncomfortable in that thing. Might as well sit here." He released her hand and shifted, leaving her space on the bed.

She hesitated, staring at the yawning space of moonlit sheet. To leave Grey if he needed her was unthinkable, but fear and uneasiness tickled down her spine. She hated that yawning fear, and it wasn't fair. She'd been happy for weeks. Happy, whole and sure of herself both as a person and as a woman. All the agony and anxiety that her ex-husband had caused her was done. Resolved. Kaput.

She just really didn't want to sit on that bed. Call it a whim or a mood. Call it that she'd acted like an absolute idiot the night before in that same bed. Call it nightmares coming out of the closet that she fiercely resented discovering now, when the real nightmare was supposed to be long over and no longer part of her life.

"You don't have to, Jill. I shouldn't have asked. I'm sorry I woke you."

"Don't be a goose." Swiftly, maybe a little awkwardly, she sank to a sitting position on top of the covers, her back straight against the headboard, her ankles crossed. "You want to talk?"

"No." He just didn't want her to leave. Twice she tried to slip out of the bed, believing him asleep. Twice his hand grabbed for hers like the bad dreams were still chasing him. How could she leave him?

Grey was beginning to despair she would ever relax when her head suddenly tilted back and her breathing evened. She never wakened when he eased her down to the pillow and worked the quilt out from under her so he could tuck it under her chin. She sighed once. He stopped dead, but the depth of her sleep was obviously real.

Silently, possessively, he tucked her back against his chest. Her hair tickled his nose; he had to smooth it down. The cast on his ankle made resting on his side less than comfortable, but sleeping spoon fashion created the most contact. He wanted the most contact, and it must have taken him ten minutes to carefully arrange it.

There was a small voice in his head that seemed to see the whole scene as a black comedy. What on earth do you think you're doing, Treveran? he thought. You can't care about this woman. You don't care about anyone or anything any more, remember?

That was true, of course. It just wasn't immediately relevant. Jill had tensed up like a coiled spring, simply because of the arm-to-arm contact on the walk home. That was immediately relevant. The woman was illogical and impractical and she offered too damn much, too freely. That was immediately relevant. The images of her bastard of an ex-husband that swarmed in his head . . . those were immediately relevant.

He didn't want Jill sleeping alone, it was that simple. He wanted her warm, close and protected, where he could keep an eye on her. He knew someone would be there if she woke up, shook up from a bad dream or bad memories. He didn't want her afraid of anything. Not tonight.

You're being illogical, Treveran, he told himself.

It worried him that he was beginning to be as batty as she was. Maybe insane thinking was catching.

The idea was terrifying.

Not so terrifying that he didn't snuggle an arm under her breasts and instantly fall asleep.

Five

Eyes still closed, Jill was suddenly aware of a sunlit morning, birdsong in the woods... and that she was snuggled closer to Grey than peanut butter and jelly.

She told herself that shock and anxiety were causing the immediate rise of her blood pressure. Unfortunately, it was too early in the morning to lie to herself. Waking up nestled against Grey felt good. Better than good. It felt right.

No memories intruded on those first moments of waking. It was too early for nightmares, too early for rational thinking. Slowly, she let the sensations unfold like fingers loosening from an invisible fist. Her thigh was wedged between his and her breasts were cuddled against his chest as if they belonged there. The smell of his sleep-warm skin and the intimate press of his arousal sent potent messages to her bloodstream.

Desire could be a soft thing. Desire could be secret and sweet and incredibly powerful. At least it was for Jill with Grey. There had to be a reason that this man and no other touched off dynamite for her. His eyes? His smile? The way he breathed?

Abruptly she realized that he was awake and must have been for some time. His voice was a murmur but it held no trace of sleepiness. "I've never met a more brazen, wanton snuggler, Jill."

An odd tightness welled in her throat. His tender words were enough to cause a new set of soft explosions and intimate feminine fires, but this was a rational world. In a rational world a woman had to know something about survival and self-protection. "Treveran."

"Hmm?"

"Would you kindly raise your right arm?"

"Right now?"

"Right now," she affirmed. When he raised it, she pushed her nightshirt down to modesty length under the covers. The lower parts of their bodies were still molded like glue and her leg was still trapped between his. "Now would you lift your right leg?"

"In a minute, Jill."

"I think immediately would be very nice."

"I think that women who wake up criminally fast should be outlawed in Tennessee."

"Maybe we could discuss that after you move your leg."

But he didn't. Instead, her head cradled back in the crook of his arm when he tilted her chin up. Whiskers darkened his jaw and his skin had a sleep glow, but Jill noticed immediately that something was wrong with his eyes. His eyes were always snapping alert in the morning. Waking was always a slam of reality for Grey. He acted as if he was bracing himself before life started stalking him again.

Not today. His eyes were dangerously dark and distinctly possessive as they lazily traveled over her tumble of hair and flushed face. He didn't seem the least interested in a sunlit morning. A velvet-yellow finch was perched on the window; he didn't seem to notice that, either. The way he looked at her made heat cluster in the lower part of her body. "You slept well," he murmured. "Did you notice?"

"I . . . yes."

"And I'm aroused as hell, Jill. Did you notice that, too?"

She needed coffee before she answered that question.

"I'm aroused," he continued in the same tone he might have used to discuss the weather, "but nothing happened last night. I had—and am having—a rather violent, wild, passionate desire to make love to you. But you might notice very carefully, honey—no one's coming on to you like a freight train, even if the inclination is there."

"Grey?"

"Hmm?"

Her lungs were having extreme difficulty remembering to haul in air, when all he was doing was weaving strands of her hair between his fingers. "Was one of us," she asked delicately, "by some remote chance trying to play amateur psychologist last night? Like by faking a lot of extraordinary pain?"

"Much more important," Grey informed her, "is that you can't get out of this bed until I get my morning kiss."

"Obviously one of us is regressing to four years old."

"Obviously."

"Would you please move your leg?"

"No."

Jill said patiently, "You have an extremely vulnerable ankle, cuts and bruises all over your body and a good-sized welt on your forehead. I mean let's get serious, sweets. A newborn kitten could escape this bed any time she wanted to."

"Yes." He tried a more conversational tone. "Kisses used to please you, until the night before last. You used to throw them around like confetti. You're a born toucher."

"You're not."

"I never have been," he agreed, "but I want my kiss."

"For the record, I was never overly impressed with blackmail or bullies."

Grey's smile died, yet his thumb brushed across her cheek with unbearable tenderness. "You're afraid of kisses—with me? I don't believe it."

"I'm not afraid!"

"So show me."

When she surged off the pillow, it was only because she was thoroughly irritated with him. Dare games were for children. All she intended was to jam a kiss on his lips and fly; she accomplished the jam of a kiss, but flying...somehow she didn't.

A frown chased across her brow as she lifted her head. She might as well have been kissing ice. As fast as he felt the touch of her mouth, his leg freed hers and his arms released their hold. The raw boldness of desire was in his eyes, but his tone was a whisper, gentle, quiet. "That's all. That's all I wanted you to know— that I wasn't going to press you, force you, hurt you. Ever, Jill."

"I never thought you were."

"You were afraid of me the other night."

She shook her head fiercely, as if that could stop the thick feeling of wanting to cry. "Not of you."

"Then of what?"

"I don't know."

"Tell me, honey."

"I don't know!"

"Jill, you can't bottle it up forever—"

Blind, fast, she buried her hands in his hair and lowered her mouth on his, silencing him in a way that nothing else could. She didn't want to talk. She couldn't talk, and Grey was wrong. Certain emotions had to be bottled away where they were bearable, escapable. But that had nothing to do with Grey or anything she'd ever felt for him.

She took his mouth like she could erase the past, the future, all that reality Grey understood too well. Her kisses were fierce, wild, wanton. His shoulder had the glaze of sunlight. She kissed that glaze. The pulse in his throat was throbbing. She kissed that pulse. The taste of him lingered in her mouth, like the taste of something sweet and incomparably special. She wanted that taste.

She wanted to give him something that mattered—the honesty of what she felt for him, the magic so real in her heart, the sweep of emotions so powerful they didn't have to have a name. Her feelings had nothing to do with Michael, with another man, or with anything that had ever happened to her. This was between Grey and her and a sunlit morning. Nothing else was going to intrude, because she wasn't going to let it.

"Easy, love, easy." His palms framed her face, holding her still. His lips suddenly hovered over hers like a promise, like a dare. His tongue traced her upper lip, then her lower one, then danced in to touch her tongue tip and withdraw. "Not desperate, honey. Soft. Soft like only you can be. Everything's going to be all right, Jill. No one's going to hurt you."

The scold in his voice was a whisper of spring wind. She ached suddenly, inside, outside, all over. This man, her man, her Grey who claimed to care for nothing and no one, was vital and vibrant and alive with caring. For her. The sweep of his fingertips, the satin black of his eyes, the tension controlled in his body with one long shudder, told her so.

Her lips touched his again, coaxing his desire, inviting a flood of it. Her hands shimmered over his skin, friction hot, restless. Her lips tempted. Her fingers wooed. She wanted to give him everything. He needed to feel loved and wanted. She loved him. She wanted him. How could anything be wrong?

His skin turned hot; she didn't know when. His eyes darkened. There was a moment when Grey's mouth trailed down and tenderly, carefully, tested the flavor of the skin on her collarbone. "Be sure," he whispered hoarsely. "Be sure you want this, because, honey..."

She knew he was warning her, but she was sure this was right. And to tell him, she let her breasts drag against him and her thighs brush his. Like a man tested beyond endurance, his kisses suddenly turned earthy, wild, potent. His palm pushed up her nightshirt and swept over bare breast, side, hips.

She'd always guessed Grey would be a demanding lover, but she hadn't known that the wet caress of his tongue on her breast would send an explosion of helplessness flooding through her. His hand slid down her abdomen to the soft nest of hair between her legs. Control was slipping from her. A sweet wild song overpowered her. She hadn't expected the heat. She hadn't expected that another human being on earth could make her soul feel this bare, this naked, this open, this...crushable.

And there it was again. Dread pooled in her stomach like panic, and with it memories of another time, a fire of pain and the horror of being totally defenseless. Her heartbeat suddenly roared in her ears; salt stung behind her closed eyelids.

"It's all right. It's all right." A tight shudder of control tightened Grey's body. She felt his fingers, not quite steady, trying to smooth back her hair. "Oh, honey, I never meant to rush you. I never meant for it to go this far. You're beautiful and you're precious and I lost my head and I'm sorry."

Her voice was as thick as the tears in her eyes. "It's not you. It's me." Words had to slip back the thick ball in her throat. "And I don't believe I did this to you twice. Teasing a man is pretty sick. Whether you believe it or not, I never—" She heard him take in air on an angry rush.

"That's not what happened and you know it." He hesitated. "You're sensitive and giving and loving, Jill, and I don't have to know what the bastard did to you to understand that you were hurt very badly. If you could try and talk about it—"

"No." The word was a snap from her soul. Grey's eyes, his soft, rolling tenor, his closeness, were suddenly an unbearable temptation to fall apart in little pieces. He was the wounded one. He was the one who needed understanding and someone to listen, and it suddenly seemed to Jill that all she'd ever done for him was embroil him in her own emotional heartache. It was unforgivable. She escaped his arms and jerked awkwardly out of bed. "I'm sorry, Grey." There was nothing else to say.

Within seconds, she was out of his room, out of the hall and into her own bedroom behind a closed door.

She shut off her mind like she would shut off an open faucet. She didn't want to think; she didn't want to feel. And she certainly didn't want to cry. Innocuously cheerful sunshine filtered through the windows, as it should. This was a plain old ordinary morning.

On plain old ordinary mornings, she got dressed. Her fingers lingered on shorts and a top, then moved swiftly to a different drawer. Unlike any other morning, she slipped on a scooped-neck top, a cotton skirt with ruffled lace at the bottom and sandals. She changed her earrings, added jewelry at her throat and wrists, reached for a brush, and moments later applied lipstick.

None of her actions required any thought. She'd found a lost man, taken him in, and fallen in love with him. That hadn't taken any thought, either. What was there to think about? He was a treasure. She'd never met a human being more responsive to caring and contact than Grey. From the very first, the need she'd seen in Grey had touched her like a sky full of fragile color in a sunrise.

Wonderful, Jill. Only you've been playing with that man's life and emotions, when you can't even handle your own. How could you do that to him?

She pushed the lipstick top back on the tube, opened the door and strode for the kitchen. Grey was already there, mixing a bowl of nuts and raisins when she knew he absolutely hated raisins. His chest was still bare, his hair still rumpled, and the way he stared at her with his soft, dark eyes fastened on her didn't help anything. Faster than he could draw breath, she stubbornly announced, "I'm leaving."

He said absolutely nothing, which was fine by Jill. There were so many terribly important things to do all at once. Wolf was whining; she had to fill the dog's dish. Then there was the business of finding her purse—since she rarely needed it here, she inevitably forgot where she stashed it.

The whole time she was whisking around the kitchen, she was talking at the speed of sound, bright, light and easy. "I won't be gone forever, just a few hours. I've needed to take the boat into Raider's Cove for days—I have phone calls to make, packages needing to be shipped out and supplies to buy. Raider's isn't much of a town, but it has a general store. Since Root's been so lazy about towing your boat I thought I'd pick you up some supplies. It's probably driven you crazy, having to borrow my toothbrush."

She finally found her crocheted purse in the bottom shelf in the hutch, which was about when she ran out of excuses to avoid looking at him. He had leaned back against the table, silent, and all she could think of was that he'd grown taller and stronger in a matter of days.

"No matter what you think you're afraid of," he said quietly, "you're a beautiful woman, Jill. Strong, whole, giving. Real. You don't have to run away from anything."

"I'm not running. I've had to make this trip for a week—"

"All right."

"I told you—"

"I heard you."

Allowing her to leave was the hardest thing he'd ever done, and the minute Jill's battered Cris-Craft left the dock, Wolf started to howl. The mutt didn't let up for two and a half hours. Grey tried hand feeding her dog food, he tried bribing her with the cookies Jill hid in the top cupboard of the hutch, and he tried scolding. The dog was inconsolable.

The only thing that even momentarily quieted the dog was petting her stomach. Grey didn't mind when a few minutes stretched into a long half hour, but when he heard his own voice crooning sweet nothings to the mutt, he thought, this is crazy.

The dog was crazy. Living in a cabin with weeds hanging from every ceiling was crazy. Love potions were crazy. Beyond anything else, allowing himself to fall in love with Jill was impossible.

She needed a lover, nothing more, nothing less. The right man in Jill's life would know what to do to help her talk, help her deal with what the bastard she'd been married to had done to her, share what was painful and ease it.

Grey had no illusions. He wasn't the right man. His own life had been an unqualified disaster since last spring. He had no idea what he was going to do, where he was going to go, how he was going to live. Nothing had dented the dark hole in his heart from the time he'd given up medicine.

The look in her eyes when she left was still tearing at him. She'd looked fragile, stubborn, proud and don't-touch-me crushable. He knew the whimsical Jill who made love potions, and the illogical Jill who loved to disturb him. He knew the woman with the healing hands and the voice like magic. But he didn't recognize this Jill. Grey had no belief in spells whatsoever, yet that was exactly what she'd done—cast spells, tangled him up in her magic, lured him into reaching out for life and emotions again.

He'd reached out, all right. And failed her.

Yesterday, the thought had idled through his mind that he might take her up on her offer to temporarily stay a little longer. He thought he could help her. Now, it was more than obvious that every time he tried to help, he hurt her.

When Root brought his houseboat, he was gone. Leaving was best for him, and definitely best for her. And that was that.

The motor sputtered and died. The boat promptly bobbed and swelled in the Tennessee River, perfectly content to drift aimlessly under a cloudless blue sky.

Jill wasn't. With a sigh, she moved from the pilot's chair back to the outboard motor. Her feet were bare, her shoes discarded the instant she left Raider's Cove. The sun beat down on her. She grabbed a rag and glared at the carburetor. Over the past three months, others had tried to fix it. The owner of the bait shop, Mr. Jenkins, had even claimed he'd done the job. Jill could have told all of them that the carburetor simply didn't want to be fixed. It liked to be coddled, sworn at, fussed over and babied.

She coddled, swore, fussed and babied. Her mood was inexplicably irritable, considering that her trip to Raider's Cove couldn't have been more successful.

She'd sent off her soaps, set up in Mrs. Jenkins's kitchen with the good lady's homemade cookies and a telephone, and contacted the three additional stores she'd been hoping to sell products to. Based on samples she'd sent them, two had immediately placed orders, and the UPS office—a tiny square of the general store—had been holding packages for her. Now the boat was loaded with boxes, filled with everything from salt and flour to books and paper. One huge carton held the tiny decorated boxes she packed her soap in. An artist friend in Atlanta had designed the boxes, and Jill had been waiting for the carton to arrive for weeks.

In short, the whole day had gone beautifully and now even the motor coughed to obedient life. "Good girl," Jill murmured, but the ragtail irritable mood wouldn't leave her.

She wanted to get home, that was all. A few hours away from Grey had given her exactly what she'd hoped for—perspective and a chance to think.

Grey couldn't stay. She'd been crazy to ask him to. Whatever was wrong in his life wasn't her problem, and interfering do-gooders had always grated on Jill. She'd never intended to interfere so much as help a man who seemed to desperately need it. Only he needed help from a woman who couldn't manage her own emotional life like he needed another broken ankle.

The best thing she could do for Grey—once Root brought his boat and he got a little steadier on his feet—was kick him out of the nest. That decision was fine, but she wanted to be home and have the issue talked over and settled.

She slowed her boat, watching for the huge overhanging branches that obscured her turnoff. The Tennessee River abounded with coves and creeks and hideaway inlets like hers, wild land that people had either forgotten about or simply never found. Three months ago she'd believed it an ideal place to get lost.

A small, nagging voice in her head whispered that she was still hiding. *Damn it, that's not fair.* Confusion and despair had been riddling her conscience since this morning. Was she sick? Would another woman have more easily been able to forget an ugly memory of violence and just gone on? Damn it, she'd tried to go on. She valued courage and she valued strength.

She also valued not hurting other people. Encouraging a man to believe you cared and then slamming a door in his face was exactly how she defined hurting Grey. It couldn't happen again.

The turnoff was in front of her. The inlet stretched for unknown miles like a splayed palm, fingers of water leading in different directions. She took the ring-finger fork into her swimming creek and slowed the motor to a putter.

Heat clustered in pockets under the trees. Jungle-like brush tangled on the opposite shore. Dragonflies played near the banks, and she caught a glimpse of silverweed—one of the most nourishing survival roots there was. She thought, I have to remember where those grow, and then abruptly glimpsed something white and huge through the branches.

Yards closer, she identified a gleaming houseboat and Root's faithful river craft. Both were moored to her dock, but no one was in sight. It didn't take much intuition for Jill to guess that Root had arrived and gone in search of her or Grey.

She cut the motor, grabbed the ropes and secured her aging Cris-Craft, barely able to keep her eyes from the houseboat. She told herself that the change in her pulse was due to relief that Root had finally brought Grey's boat, making it possible for Grey to leave as soon as he wanted.

Still, she frowned as she leapt barefoot to the narrow wooden dock and padded toward the larger craft. She'd seen houseboats before, and this was no larger than most—about fifty feet—but it was loaded with luxuries. The back deck held a gas grill and lounge chairs deep and thick enough to sleep in. Although the sun obscured her vision, she could see a long couch and thick pile carpeting through the glass doors leading to the main cabin.

She didn't necessarily set foot on the boat because of curiosity. The boat would need airing out before he could use it, didn't it? All closed up, the air inside would be stifling.

It was stifling, and a rotten smell assailed her as she pushed open the doors. The main cabin was both living room and kitchen, and beyond was a bedroom with two massive, bunked double beds and a bath. She only glanced around quickly. The rotten smells emanating from the refrigerator were too pervasive to be ignored.

She threw open every window she could before peering into the fridge. It was certainly chock-full, but almost everything in it was spoiled. Searching for a plastic bag, her eyes lingered on the microwave, color TV and marble-topped table. A man without income couldn't have rented this boat for a day, much less a couple of months.

She threw out the dead lettuce, sandwich meat, six steaks—Lord, that was criminal!—three bowls of different kinds of fruit and a pile of vegetables. By the time she was twisting a wrap on the plastic bag, her heart was beating like a ticker-tape machine. The refrigerator was functioning. Four or five days wasn't enough to spoil so much food . . . unless a man simply hadn't been eating for a long time before that.

She straightened, shoving her hair back. The creek breeze was fast rushing through the open windows and doors, but it wasn't enough to immediately dissipate the bad smells and heat. Her nape was damp and her hair was coming down. She should leave.

She didn't. The color TV wasn't plugged in and the counters were spotless. No books were out, no open magazines. The sinks were clean and neither bed looked slept in. It was as if no one had ever lived here.

After five minutes, most people found a way to clutter up a place. What the devil had Grey done, sat there in a chair and brooded the whole time he'd traveled in the damn thing?

Jill, he's not yours to worry about, she reminded herself. You can't help a man when you can't even help yourself. When are you going to get that through your head?

"Jill!"

She pivoted at the sound of Grey's voice and rushed to the open front deck. Grey was hobbling down her rickety dock like a man who thought he could run races. Root was ambling behind him.

She only saw Grey. Embarrassed, she justified her nosiness: "I was just throwing out some food—there was a terrible smell."

"I'll take care of any problems that are in there."

"Fine. I was just trying to help."

"I don't need help. Anyone's help."

"Fine," she repeated more slowly. She'd left him in a reasonable mood; obviously something had turned it to mud. Not your business, she reminded herself, and didn't say a single word when he stumbled on a loose board. He was a grown man with eyes, and he already knew her dock was on the perilous side of rickety.

Root shouted out a peaceable hello and Wolf stood at the banks, violently wagging her tail.

"Hi, baby!"

"That dog—" Grey started gruffly.

She whirled. ''There's nothing wrong with that dog.''

''She howled the whole time you were gone.''

''Is that my fault?''

''It sure as hell isn't mine.''

She clenched her teeth, not because he was being insufferably rude but because the leap from dock to boat was too much for him. The stupid man! Now sweat was breaking out all over his forehead; he'd probably half killed himself and his ankle, too.

''Look, I could have gotten clothes for you,'' she started reasonably.

''I'll get clothes—enough for today. I won't need more than that.''

''Oh?''

''I'll be leaving in the morning.'' His eyes flashed a challenge before he moved past her into the bedroom cabin.

Her pulse stopped pounding and fell like a stone to the bottom of the river. She said briskly, ''If you feel up to it.''

''I feel up to it.''

Enough was enough. ''Do you also feel up to having your block knocked off? Because if you snap at me one more time, Treveran, that's exactly what's going to happen.''

Seconds later he appeared between the bedroom and main cabin with clothes and toiletry supplies stashed under an arm. Something had changed in those few seconds. He no longer looked nasty, just unbearably exhausted and frustrated. His voice had changed from a snap to a slow, rolling tenor. "I'm sorry, Jill. I didn't mean to snap at you."

What was it about this man? He breathed. She melted. "It's all right."

"It's just…we both know it's time I was gone. I've taken advantage of your hospitality long enough. I haven't had a fever in twenty-four hours. Maybe I'm not up to the Olympics but I can easily manage in this little space." He hesitated. "I really don't know how to thank you for all you've done."

"You don't need to thank me. Here, let me take those clothes." It occurred to her that he'd only been impatient and brusque because he had his mind on leaving her. He probably couldn't wait to leave her. When it came down to it, she couldn't wait for him to leave. Everything was working out beautifully, except that her heart felt like lead and her stomach refused to stop sinking.

"I can carry everything," Grey insisted. "And it looks like you brought a boat loaded with supplies to take up to the house."

"Root'll help. For that matter, nothing's heavy, just bulky. Seriously, Grey, let me take those things in your arms. It's hard enough for you to get in and out of the boat—"

"Look, damn it, I'm nobody's parasite. I can handle it."

One minute he was talking, fumbling with his walking crutch and the clothes in his arms and the rail on the boat. The next instant he was in midair. She heard his groan of pain just before he disappeared from sight.

Before she even heard the splash, she moved faster than lightning, faster than jets, faster than sound. The creek was shallow near shore, but the end of her long dock was rooted in deep water. From the corner of her eye she saw Root peeling off his boots, but she wasn't about to wait for him.

Cold water closed over her head like a shock of ice. Her bare foot touched bottom and she used that momentum to surge to the surface again. Grey wasn't three feet from her—he'd surfaced, too—but at a glance she could see the gash in his temple was bleeding, and God knew how heavy the ankle cast was in water.

He was heaving in air, sputtering water, trying to dog paddle, trying to talk—mostly trying to swear and yell something about how all right he was. All she saw was the blood on his forehead, and she could only think that there was going to be more, because she was going to kill him. But not quite yet.

His clothes were floating downstream; so was a toothbrush. Root splashed through the shallows, overalls and all, and then waited just at the drop-off to deep water. Jill surged toward Grey, wrapped an arm around his chest and pulled him sidestroke toward the shallower water.

Root had a hold on him in seconds. He reached under Grey's shoulders while she reached for his thighs so Grey couldn't stand on the ankle. A beached whale would have been easier to lift to the dock. The whole rescue couldn't have taken five minutes. The whole time Root was yelling and Grey was yelling and the dog was howling.

Jill had been absolutely silent until she really looked at him. Streaks of red were dancing on his forehead under the sun. He'd scraped his back. The wooden cast was soaked, and she had no idea what water had done to his broken ankle.

Swear words weren't usually her cup of tea, but she used a slew of them now. "That's it! I don't care about this morning; I don't care about anything. You hear me, Treveran? You're staying, you big stupid lummox, and I don't want to hear another word about it! If you seriously hurt yourself, you're going to be sorry you were ever born. Go ahead! Argue with me!"

Grey wasn't inclined to argue, and suddenly Root was very busy, checking the damage to his wet corncob pipe.

Six

Jill hadn't remembered the supplies she'd left in her boat until after dinner. Grey knew that hauling the boxes from the dock would take her some time.

Before she'd left the house, she'd made absolutely sure that he couldn't help her. Grey cast a narrowed eye at the torture device she had set up for him. Right after his dip in the creek, his ankle had started to swell. Jill's concept of traction was to rig sheets to the ceiling beams. His leg was trussed in the make-shift swing, and grudgingly Grey was willing to admit that her concept worked. Jill was outstanding at immobilizing a man. She'd also left him a baby-sitter.

The old codger was in the rocker, whittling a piece of wood with a jackknife. Neither he nor Grey had

had the chance to say much over the past three hours. They'd both been stripped of wet clothes, fed, re-clothed and snapped at for even the mildest attempt to interject something peaceable in the conversation. Jill in a temper had something in common with a full-power tornado.

Grey cleared his throat, more to break the silence than anything else. "You wouldn't like to try and rea-son with her, would you?"

"Jill?" Root only momentarily lifted his knife, as if to seriously consider the question. "Nope, I wouldn't want to try and reason with Jill."

"It would be best for her if I left," Grey said qui-etly.

"Could be I thought the same thing when I first met her." Mistrustful eyes lanced on Grey, then softened. "Could be I had an idea or two you'd hurt Jill. And could be, it's possible for a body to occasionally change their mind."

"Could be—" Grey dryly echoed his Tennessee twang "—that you're certainly singing a different tune than you were this afternoon. Before Jill got back, you seemed to have a lot to say about a man who'd take advantage of a woman living alone and vulnerable."

"I was just passing the time with that conversa-tion." The piece of wood in Root's hand was begin-ning to shape into a duck's head. "Course, that was afore how I saw how you two was together this after-noon. You done a lot for her."

"I haven't done anything—but be in her way and upset her."

"I think she'd see that different."

"I don't."

"I sure ain't gonna argue with you all night about it," Root said peaceably.

The room folded in silence again, a silence that annoyed Grey. He should have appreciated the peace. He was exhausted. He really didn't need the new collection of aches and bruises he'd accumulated that afternoon. And the room was gradually darkening with the hushed, soothing stillness of sunset. Silence was golden, but it just didn't seem the same without Jill in it. "It would be different if I knew the right things to say to her," he mentioned to the ceiling.

"Never knew a man alive knew the right things to say to a woman," Root concurred mildly. He started carving the duck's wing. "Guess by now you figured out she was once hooked up with a rattlesnake. Zapped her with poison, he did. A certain kind of venom can be real tough to get out of a body's system. But then you'd know all about a body's system, wouldn't you?"

"I beg your pardon?"

"You don't have to go beggin' no pardon of mine," Root assured him, and concentrated head-down on his whittling. "You tole her you're a healing man yet?"

"What?" Grey's eyes whipped to Root's face. "Where on earth did you get that idea?"

"Weren't hard." Root took a short break, surveying his artwork. "Didn't know for sure till I saw you looking at Hiram's knee the other day, but I guessed afore that. Never met a body wasn't scared of the unknown. Rich man like you, wake up injured real bad, pain driving you darn near crazy—seems to me you should have been scared, see, seems to me that the only thing in your head should have been climbing into a nice fancy civilized hospital bed. Instead, you don't even show a whit of worry about what's wrong with you. Course you wouldn't 'a been worried. If you already knew exactly what was wrong."

"I'm not a doctor." It was the first time Grey had said the words aloud.

"Have it your own way. Sure don't matter to me." Root peered at the table beside Grey's bed. "If I was you, I'd worry less about what you was and wasn't and worry more about finishing that tea afore she gets back. No sense heaping more trouble on your head."

Grey was glad to change the subject. "You've never tasted Jill's teas."

"Ah." Root's bones creaked as he lurched out of the rocker. The pockets in his wrinkled, patched overalls were as big as suitcases. One yielded a small glass flask. "This is good Tennessee corn brew, and I wouldn't be offerin' it to just anybody. I've had to doctor a few of Jill's teas myself."

The first sip burned Grey's throat. The second acted like a fast-acting pain pill, and the third took all the sharpness out of the shadows. When he finished the first mug, Root poured him another. "We don't," Grey suggested carefully, "necessarily need to tell Jill about this."

"Lots of things Jill don't need to know," Root agreed.

Root was waiting in the doorway for Jill when she headed up the porch with her arms full of boxes. "Sleeping like a bear in hibernation," he told her in a whisper. "Won't need to check on him the whole rest of the night."

"He didn't try to climb out of the traction?"

"Nope."

"Did he drink the tea?"

"Every drop. I jes don't understand all you been saying about him, Jill. That boy's no problem to handle atall."

"Oh, Lord. He must be really ill," Jill said swiftly. She dropped the boxes and would have rushed through the bedroom doorway if Root hadn't been planted there.

"Now, Jill, I swear he's resting just fine. He needs rest and you need rest and I can't think of a thing on this green earth that needs any more worrying until morning."

"You're sure he's fine?"

"Dead sure."

But she shook her head, trying to peer past him. "You don't know Grey like I do. I—"

Root heaved an arm around her shoulder and led her toward the kitchen. "Tell you what I'm goin' to do. I'm going to make you a little mug of tea afore I go. One, maybe two. Same kind of tea you brewed for him, accepting that I'm going to add something real special to yours—a real natural herbal ingredient that grows right under this Tennessee sun. Guaranteed to give a body a little perspective after a long, trying day."

Root slipped into the woods at midnight. He felt good, if a little tuckered. Both his charges had been adequately dosed with perspective and were sleeping like babies.

When Grey woke up, Jill was in his room, standing at the base of his bed in scarlet shorts and a safari-print blouse. For once the outfit was perkier than she was. Her eyelids were still heavy from dreams and the yawn that escaped her came out slow and lazy. When she realized he was awake, she perched on the end of the bed and stretched out her long brown legs, eyes on her bare toes. "G'morning."

"Morning," he echoed.

"Nice day."

"Seems that way." Amused, Grey watched her inspect a knee as if it might have become deformed over the night. He could have told her it was a perfectly lovely knee.

"Grey?"

"Hmm?"

"How much hooch did he slip you?"

"Probably enough to go blind."

She nodded. "Next time I see that wily old coot, I'll probably shoot him." She glanced at him. "It would be a very bad idea for you to bring up the idea of your leaving this morning."

"I wasn't going to bring it up." He added, "This morning."

"How's your leg?"

"Fine."

"How's the new cast feel?"

"Fine."

"How's your head?"

"Fine."

She eased to her feet. "So what are you still doing lying in bed? About time you earned your keep, Treveran."

A week later, Grey considered the fact that she'd made it impossibly easy for him to stay. His spine was molded against a tree trunk and his fishing pole was dipped in the river. Sun dappled through the overhanging branches of the sycamore—not too much, not too little. The dancing, cool water, the cushioned grassy bank and the soporific heat made for a mesmerizing laziness. He mentally tested the rich, rare, unexpected feeling of well-being.

Fifty yards from him, Jill thought absently that this was the best of all possible worlds. The field where she was picking dandelions was open, sunlit and scented with summer. Bees hummed from the periwinkles to the daisies. A barest breeze caressed her skin. The air was fresh, clear, sweet. How could a woman not feel marvelous on a day like this?

When Grey felt the tug on his line, he eased forward, praying for a bass. Two nights in a row he'd brought home catfish. Not that Jill couldn't fillet a blade of grass and make it delectable, but he'd had it with catfish. The days had fallen into a pattern. Afternoons, he worked on bringing home dinner; mornings, he collected junk for her fool potions. He did both without complaint. In fact, he'd done everything Jill had asked him without complaint, and he'd found a thousand ways to help her that didn't include touching her. Nothing could have been easier.

Crouched down, Jill plucked another dozen dandelions, and separated the flowers from the stems because the stems were bitter. She needed four quarts of the blossoms, and so far had accumulated about three. It had been a wonderful week. She'd made soaps and cosmetic creams, gardened, entertained a dozen neighbors and enjoyed the sunshine. On a more personal level, she felt like she had the power of a female general with Grey—attacking the serious in him, planning strategies to make him strong and healthy again, maneuvering laughter out of him. If she could give Grey nothing else, she could give him these woods, time, peace. She wanted to give him those things. She was determined to give him those things.

Grey reeled in the line and, satisfied, noted the big-mouthed black bass wriggling at the end of it. The baby was a good foot in length. One more catch, and dinner would be in the pail. As he baited the hook a second time, he glimpsed Jill from the corner of his eye. The field was all color, soft-swaying motion and sunlight. It suited Jill. He could see the sun glow on her face, the tanned stretch of her bare legs under scarlet shorts, her hair catching the dance and fire of the late-afternoon sun. She moved like the wind: easy, sensual, natural. A woman like Jill, he thought disin-

terestedly, could completely annihilate a man's previous definitions of female sex appeal.

Jill stopped to rest when the pails of dandelion
blossoms were full. Lazily stretching, she caught a
peek at Grey's long legs under the tree. He'd gained
weight this week, and he'd needed it. His ankle and the
gash on his forehead couldn't heal overnight, but the
rest of his body was becoming wonderfully brown and
sleek and healthy. Virility and vitality, she thought
with critical impartiality, could be a potent combination. Some woman, sometime, was going to have the
sense to snap him up.

Grey thought, I'm about to go out of my mind.

Jill thought, This can't go on.

Grey picked up the fish bucket and reached for his
rowan walking cane. "I'm headed for the cabin," he
called to Jill.

"Me, too." Her two pails were huge but light.
Blossoms didn't weigh much. She waited as Grey ambled toward the path. "Good catch?"

"A bass for your dinner. Both fish are of a good
size."

She nodded. "If you feel up to it tomorrow, you can
collect some black mustard seeds and daisies for me."

"Sure." Neither distaste nor disgust colored his
tone. If Jill wanted daisies, he'd pick her damn daisies. "I'll be glad to."

"I thought you would."

His hands were full. He motioned with his chin toward her pails. "What are we doing with those?" He
mentally congratulated himself on the "we."

"Dandelion wine," she said blithely.

"I thought that was nothing but a country legend."

"Actually, the recipe's as old as the hills. There won't be much to do tonight. All I have to do is clean the blossoms and cover them with boiling water, and they sit like that for twenty-four hours. It's tomorrow night we'll be working on making the wine itself."

"Go ahead, Jill."

"Go ahead?"

He said patiently, "The devil's in your eyes. I've seen it before. Go ahead and tell me all the lore about dandelions."

"Well..." Her grin was as light as the breeze. "If you want to know how long you're going to live, you blow the seeds off the head of the dandelion. The number of seeds left will tell you how many years you've got left."

"How helpful," Grey murmured.

"And everyone knows that if you bury a dandelion in the northwest corner of your house, it'll bring favorable winds."

"I see."

"Dandelions are also called lion's tooth and priest's crown. Some people make coffee from dandelion roots. Some say the flowers and leaves can be made into a tea for reducing swelling in the ankles."

"And the wine?" He allowed no trace of exasperation to enter his voice.

"Is absolutely useless. I don't care for it at all, it's too strong. But my neighbors like it so I give it as a present. Root's always bringing fresh meat; Billy's mom sends me fresh eggs. The roof in the kitchen had a leak when I first moved here. The neighbors fixed it; I never had to ask. They would have been offended if I'd offered them money in payment, so I—yech!''

The nip on her ankle startled more than hurt her, but she couldn't help the yelp when a zillion yellow blossoms flew in the air. Her pails went flying and so did she. Her fanny collided with the earth in what had to be one of the most embarrassing, graceless bumps of all times.

''What on earth—''

She heard his bucket splash down behind her, but all she could see were the fallen flowers. ''All my dandelions!''

''Forget the damn flowers. What happened?''

She checked the bit of a mark on her ankle, crossly brushed the dirt from her legs and grabbed her empty pail. ''Darn thing bit me. How klutzy can you get? I—''

''Jill, shut up. *What* bit you?''

''A snake. I walked right on the poor thing.'' She shivered once, violently, and then started whisking handfuls of dandelions back in the pail. ''Can't stand snakes, never could. Living around here, you'd think I'd have the sense to look where I was going—''

''Would you stop crawling around like a two-year-old? Where?''

''Where what?'' she asked irritably. The blossoms were going to be crushed and bruised, the wine would be terrible and her rear end was stinging.

"Where were you bitten?"

"On the leg. It's nothing." Something in his tone finally filtered into her mind as wrong, off-key, out of sync. She glanced back and nearly chuckled at the drained color in Grey's face. "So you're not too fond of snakes, either? Actually, that's just good sense. The woods around here have their share of timber rattlers and cottonmouths, but this was just a little racer. They're not poisonous. They wouldn't hurt a soul unless a soul does something darn stupid like step on them."

She stopped talking and she stopped feeling inclined to chuckle. Most people had an unconscious horror of snakes, but that quick reaction wasn't fading from Grey's face. Anxiety had turned his skin white; stress darkened his eyes to jet black. "Treveran, I'm fine," she said more slowly. "She barely nicked me. It's nothing. My rear end and my pride need a lot more sympathy than my leg. Grey, for heavens' sake!"

It didn't startle her so much when he hurled his cane as when he stumbled down and grabbed her. One instant she was on all fours, the next she was sitting on a bruise. He anchored her foot on his stomach, and firm large hands were all over her leg. If his touch was gentle, his skin was ashen white.

She tried humor, slowly, carefully. "Need a magnifying glass? Two itsy-bitsy scratches. No broken skin, no blood. I really don't think we'll need to amputate. Good thing, I'm rather fond of that leg." She added, "Maybe one of us could lighten up here?"

He heard her, but she might as well have been talking to him long distance. Blood was still rushing to his head; his heart was still pounding. The momentum to grab her had not been unreasonable. Jill would coddle a bruised ant. She never paid a whit of attention to herself. The snake bite could have been serious, and it would be typical of Jill not to make much of it.

It wasn't typical of Grey to lose total control in the snap of an instant. Her calf lay between his palms, sun warm, life warm, and—as she'd said—the injury was no more than two bare scratches, but he couldn't seem to release his hold.

She was staring at him like he'd lost his mind. Maybe he had. Haunting images of a five-year-old boy kept winging through his head. A five-year-old who had died—maybe because he hadn't cared enough. Maybe because he'd been exhausted after working too many fourteen-hour days. Maybe because he wasn't a good enough doctor, a strong enough man, maybe because he'd seen too much life and death and just didn't have the perspective any more. Could he have willed that boy to live if he'd just been a better man? He'd seen others recover from diabetic comas. Just not this one. Just not the child.

How the hell could he even have considered touching Jill?

He dropped her leg like it was a hot potato and reached blindly back for his cane.

Jill, belatedly aware she had a handful of dandelions clutched in her fist, tossed them behind her. The expression in his eyes was agonizing, lost, fathomless. A sunlit path had turned into a nightmare for him, and she didn't have the least idea why. "You can just come right back here—you're going to tell me what's wrong, Grey. And right now."

"Nothing's wrong." He buried the images and hauled himself up, using the cane as a lever. His hands were slick as glass and he was furious at his own lack of control.

"You can pass off that kind of nonsense on your favorite maiden aunt. This is me, Jill. And I want to know what just happened to you."

"I get the willies over snakes."

"Try another one, Treveran."

"I have a leg fetish, and I get a little panicky at anything happening to your legs. You have nice legs. In fact, you have outstanding—"

"Grey!"

He said harshly, "Leave it alone."

She left it alone for a time because she had to. Three teenage girls were waiting when they arrived back at the cabin. The excuse for the call was that one of them was hoping for a miracle cure for a typical puberty case of acne. Jill suspected they wanted an excuse to get out of the house and talk girl talk away from their mothers' watchful eyes.

By the time Grey had skinned and filleted the fish, the girls showed no inclination to leave. Dinner stretched for five and turned into a giggly affair. Judith Webster latched on to the seat next to Grey and practiced batting her short blond lashes at him, thir-

teen-year-old style. Grey was kind, genial and easy
with all three of them. If he felt the least impatience or
stress, it didn't show.

Afterward, Jill sliced a dozen sow thistles, collected the herb's milky juice in a cup and made masks
for the girls' complexions. Shy giggling turned rowdy
before she was through, but she had the chance to talk
up the real magic in complexion care—diet and careful cleanliness. Maybe the good advice filtered through
and maybe it didn't. The girls had a good time, but Jill
knew the exact instant Grey disappeared.

It was still another half hour before she was able to
scoot the girls out the door, with Wolf as an escort
through the woods. She flipped off her apron as soon
as they were out of sight, and searched first in the
backyard, then the living room.

She found Grey in his room. It wasn't dark yet. The
sun was just beginning to lower over the treetops, but
the light in his room was pewter and the rocker in the
corner shadowed. He wasn't rocking.

She could have framed his loneliness in a picture.
Even when he'd left the kitchen, no one would ever
have guessed he was brooding. Grey never showed
moodiness; he simply withdrew. If there had been a
wall surrounding him, it would have been made of ice.

As soon as he realized she was standing there, he
instantly changed his expression and pushed at the
rocker arms to raise himself up. "You need help with
something, Jill?"

"What I need is company outside. It's just turning
cool. An ideal time to watch a sunset and sip wine, and

I don't want to do either one alone. Move your itsy-bitsy buns, sexy."

"Jill—"

"The girls are gone. You're safe," she said cheerfully. "Should have done your male ego good to have Judith stare at you like the sun rose and fell when you breathed. I'd almost forgotten how painful it is to be thirteen."

It wasn't that hard to get him outside. Grey had made a major habit of accommodating her every whim this past week. She brought the jug of violet wine and a single glass for Grey, set out two lawn chairs near the fire pit and built a small bracken fire.

By the time the fire was spitting and crackling, the vibrant colors of sunset backdropped the trees. A pair of rabbits scampered through the yard and a fawn peeked her curious head at the edge of the woods. The red sky gradually faded to that special deep blue just before the blanket of night. Darkness edged closer. The dame's rocket and bouncing bet and rosemary bushes near the cabin all came to life, their scents roused with the first promise of night dew.

The night was pure magic, if a person just had the sense to let it in. Grey might have been bullied into stretching out in the lounger but he had no such sense, which was why she leaned over and poured him a second glass of wine.

"Jill, would you quit coddling me," he said suspiciously.

"Coddling you? You're out of your tree, Treveran. I'm setting you up for a little talk, can't you tell?"

"A little talk about what?"

"The birds and the bees."

"Save your breath. My father covered that one when I was eleven."

"You're already interrupting and I haven't even gotten started," she scolded, but she waited a moment before continuing.

Ignoring the second lounge chair, Jill crossed her legs and sank next to Grey. His right thigh made a table for her elbow, and she had an excellent view of his face. Nag the man enough and inevitably his eyes lost their bleakness. Exasperation wasn't necessarily an improvement in his mood, but there was a faint—a very faint—trace of rueful humor in his expression. He was prepared to please, to listen, to accommodate. She guessed he would have attempted gymnastics to avoid upsetting her, because he'd relentlessly steered clear of any conversational subject that could have upset her all week.

She'd avoided troubled waters as carefully as he had, which was why her palms were damp and her stomach now rolling. He'd wandered into his own private hell that afternoon. Her instinct had been to touch and hold him, an instinct she'd been ignoring ever since touching Grey had become something complicated, shadowed, dangerous. An untended sliver, though, tended to fester, and she cared too much about Grey to let that happen.

"Listen, gorgeous," she said lightly, "this whole last week, you've been a marvel of a houseguest. It's worked out beautifully, hasn't it? You needed a place to recuperate; I wanted someone around. You'd think our life-styles meshed like butter on bread. If I said the moon was blue, you would have agreed, wouldn't you? And so sweet, you've collected all the ingredients for my love potions, pushed a broom before I've even made a mess, looked for ways to help before I could even think about asking. Both of us have been careful not to infringe on each other's privacy, and why should we? Talk's cheap, and we've been doing just fine without talking. Ever heard the old proverb about never disturbing sleeping bats in a cave?"

"No," he said dryly.

"Some old proverbs," Jill said firmly, "are a pile of crock. You and I will be 'just friends' on the same day it rains cats, and you might as well drink your wine and relax because I'm about to get nosy." Elbow still on his thigh, she cupped her chin in her palm. "You don't have to tell me what happened to you this afternoon, Treveran. I love guessing games, and actually, I've already done a fair amount of guessing about your life story. How about—the IRS chasing you?"

He looked as if he'd been about to say something else, but the question startled him. "No, of course not—"

"Some jealous husband unfairly blackmailing you?"

"No—"

"Some jealous husband fairly blackmailing you?"

"Jill—"

"Your business is in Chapter Eleven and the creditors were chasing you over three continents?"

"No." A chuckle flavored the word.

"Ah. You did something terrible in your misbegotten youth, and the scandal caught up with you. You made a porn flick when you were nineteen? I love that idea. Truthfully, it seems terribly out of character, but—"

"Jill. No."

"Hemorrhoids? Lethal allergies?" She wasn't totally surprised to see him drop the glass of wine and slowly, determinedly climb out of the lounger. She continued blithely, "Three women chasing after you at the same time, and it got too much? A partner cheat you blind? Stress overload? Burnout? Lord, Grey, you didn't sell secrets to the Russians, did you?"

Jill was very easy to silence. She was still crouched on her knees when Grey dropped to the grass beside her, legs splayed to make serious closeness possible. "You have," he said gravely, "a terrible habit of worrying about people."

She felt his fingers on her nape and her whole body went still. Moving was suddenly out of the question. Breathing normally was difficult. "Other people automatically bring these little tidbits into a conversation—where they're from, what they do. Not you, Treveran."

"I never had any deep dark secrets, just a problem that no one could handle but me." He hesitated, well aware that Jill's pulse was leaping beneath his palm. "Everyone makes mistakes. I made a very bad mistake that I have to learn to live with. It has nothing to do with you, honey, and it's nothing you need to worry about."

She shook her head fiercely. "Grey, you couldn't have done anything that bad."

He didn't argue with her. Talking wasn't going to change what he'd done or hadn't done on a spring night a long time ago. Right now he was too aware of her growing tension to think of anything else.

She was coiled to spring—and had been any time he'd inadvertently touched her all week. Her pulse was frantic. Color was climbing her cheeks, far more than could be caused by the glow of the fire. She was afraid to look at him. Was she wary of what he'd see in her eyes?

But he already knew how her eyes picked up the fire of emeralds whenever he looked at her a certain way. He knew that she wanted him, and that she was terrified of freezing up again.

All week he'd ignored the electricity that crackled whenever they were in the same room. All week he'd respected Jill's choices, and those included establishing distance from a relationship she didn't want. Lord knew he was the wrong lover for her. He knew exactly how little he had to offer Jill, long term, short term, any term.

But she was trembling.

Abruptly, Grey discovered that he had lost all tolerance for Jill trembling because of him, which was why that first kiss was absolutely, irrevocably, inarguably necessary.

Seven

Jill had ample time to step away. She could see the intent in Grey's eyes even before his lips hovered over and sank onto hers. All week she'd battened down all feelings of desire, want and need for him. She'd been too worried she would freeze up on him again to encourage even the slightest contact. She didn't want to do that to him. She didn't want to do it to herself.

But the taste of him flooded her senses. The rub of his lips on hers wooed her heart and her head. In another minute, she promised herself, she'd stop this. She'd almost gotten him talking, and he was mistaken if he believed he could divert her with a little physical intimacy. Frankly, kissing her was an unscrupulous, dishonorable, unfair thing to do. She wasn't going to forgive him.

His thumb traced the line of her cheekbone. The fingers of his other hand threaded through her hair; his tongue teased the seam of her lips until she opened her mouth. She wasn't going to forgive him for those things, either.

Embers crackled behind them. The whispered sounds of night closed them in. She could smell sweet green grass and rosemary. Grey had a wicked, wicked tongue, a tongue that should be outlawed. As long as she didn't respond, of course, there could be no problem. She stayed on her knees, immobile, patient, her hands locked on her lap as carefully as a duchess taking tea.

His lips trailed into her hair, dawdled on the shell of her ear, lost themselves in the hollow of her throat. Jill discovered a small problem maintaining the demeanor of a duchess. She felt fragile where Grey kissed her. Her skin felt like silk. Possibly...possibly...Grey made the stars shine. That was another thing she wasn't going to forgive him for.

When his lips were busy on her throat, she remembered her voice. "Grey?"

"Hmm?"

"We gave this kind of thing up last week, remember?"

"I remember every mistake I've ever made in this life," he assured her.

"It's getting cold—"

"It's hot," he corrected her.

"Mosquitoes—"

"Your fire wards off mosquitoes, remember?" He smiled at her as he hadn't smiled at anyone in the last thousand years. While her gaze was pinned on his smile, he slowly eased the buttons loose from her blouse. "I'm going to make love to you, Jill."

She stopped breathing. The night air tickled across her skin when he slid the blouse from her shoulders. She couldn't seem to stop gazing into his eyes, and she felt herself falling as Grey eased her down into the grass. She made a valiant effort to sound normal. "I don't necessarily think that's such a terrific idea."

"I do." Lowering his head, he nuzzled the curve of her throat. The firelight gave her breasts a pearl glow next to the blade-green grass. His lips skimmed from her throat to the first swell of her breasts, and he heard her breath catch.

"I . . . don't want to start something. I'll just panic again."

"Not this time."

"Grey, there's nothing different about this time."

"Yes, there is. Because when you run this time, I'm going to be there to catch you."

His voice sounded quiet and easy and sure. With equal sureness, she felt the gentle tug of his teeth on her nipple and came close to completely unraveling. His hands swept over her flesh with an urgency and speed that made her blood thicken and heat. She made a restless move to stop his hands from unlatching the button of her shorts, and he abruptly loomed over her and dropped a fierce, scolding kiss on her lips.

Obviously he'd turned into someone else. This wasn't Grey. Grey wasn't... aggressive, impatient, demanding. All the dynamics of darkness and desire had been there before; he'd never pressed. He'd never once shown less than patience and control and sensitivity to her feelings. All this time she'd been safe with Grey.

At the moment she felt as safe as a leaf in a hurricane. She seemed to be becoming bare, very fast. Firelight illuminated his face, all unyielding bones and uncompromising planes as he pushed the shorts down her thighs. If he'd smile she'd feel safe, but he wasn't smiling. His eyes had turned liquid, dangerously intense, blacker than midnight.

"Undo my shirt, honey." He raised her hand to the first button, and used his fingers to guide her when her own faltered. When the buttons were undone, he shook off the shirt and hurled it, startling her. The motion was almost violent, which did nothing for her accelerating heartbeat. "Now touch," he ordered softly.

The grass crinkled beneath her and the night's humidity was unbearably pervasive. She could feel tendrils of hair clinging to her nape. Beneath her palm, Grey's skin had something in common with dynamite. The slightest brush of her hands, and every muscle in his body tightened. The simplest dance of her fingertips, and he flexed like a lightning bolt had shot through him. She could feel sinewed hardness beneath skin. She touched rough hair and smooth flesh. And the whole time she couldn't look away from his eyes.

Her voice was a helpless whisper. "I think that you're deliberately trying to make me afraid."

"A little." He broke the eye contact when he ducked his head. His rough-whiskered chin scraped against her throat as he moved his free leg between hers, holding her, trapping her. "Do you feel vulnerable, honey?"

"Yes." His arousal was like steel, even through his jeans. She could hardly be more intimately aware of it.

"You're going to feel more vulnerable. Because I'm going to taste every inch of your skin and I'm going to kiss you until you can't breathe and I'm going to take you. Slow and hard."

He peppered kisses on her mouth, one after the other, until dark sensations were singing through her body, rippling along the surface of her skin. Her breasts ached, swollen with a sudden heaviness under the caress of his tongue. The lower part of her body filled up with pressure. She was standing at the edge of a precipice. The feeling was heady and exciting and exhilaratingly special. But there was a nightmare quality to it, too. She didn't want to fall.

"Let it go, Jill," he whispered.

"I can't!"

"Yes, you can." He wanted to give her soft, tender, gentle. He couldn't. Since murmured words seemed to shake her, he used them. His tongue on her nipple made her heart pound. The sweep of his palm on the inside of her thigh made her buck toward him. She cried out his name when he nipped at her throat.

His jeans were the only clothing that lay between them. The night was still hot and the fire crackled and spit. All he saw was Jill, a woman with silver-green eyes lost somewhere between a promise and a nightmare. She undoubtedly believed there was no other thought in his head but to take her.

"Let it go, honey," he whispered again.

Blinding tears stung her eyes. Restless and angry, her hands roamed his back, his sides, anywhere she could touch. Rage spilled out of her for emotions she couldn't control, for memories she couldn't erase. Like fine crystal, she was afraid of shattering. Like the sweep of wind in a storm, she was afraid of yielding.

His mouth took hers over and over. She grappled for control that was slipping away from her. His hot, slick skin and brazen arousal pressed against her. His hands wooed her and she felt his sinewed thighs. Grey was merciless, a man who would steal a woman's basic defenses, a man who had no intention of giving her choices.

"Oh, sweetheart, let it go!" he urged again.

He suddenly wrapped her so close, so hard, so tightly. She held on to him, but not by choice. He was her only raft in a huge dark ocean, and the words rushed out of her in a helpless flood. "It's this…it was always this. I'm not afraid of you; it's me, it's me. I can't be defenseless again, can you understand? I can't. I have to be able to protect myself. It's survival. I was vulnerable once, defenseless once. And when you touch me, that's how I feel again, only worse, Grey, worse."

She was shaking so hard. He cradled, soothed, rocked her, but not for long. He intended to hear all of what had happened to her with her ex-husband. But not right away. The only thing that mattered was what Jill was now feeling, and talking up the past wasn't going to cross that bridge. "You so badly want those feelings to disappear," he whispered fiercely. "I don't, honey. I want you to feel vulnerable. I want you to feel defenseless. I want your fear; I want every hurt you've ever had, every emotion you've ever felt. I want you to yield . . . everything. Do it for me. You think I'd let anything in hell hurt you? Do it, honey, do it."

A devil fire took her, then a wash of trembling, but Grey knew the exact moment she yielded. *"Yes,"* he whispered. Her kisses flowed over him like smooth dark honey, and then he felt her fingers digging into the rich thickness of his hair. Perhaps it rained diamonds. He couldn't have cared. Her eyes went lush and soft and he could taste yearning on her tongue. *I'll make this right for you, Jill.*

He stripped off his jeans, impatient with the cast, impatient with anything that separated him from Jill for even seconds. She was beautiful, golden, slender, vital. She'd always been magic for him, but never more than now.

He kissed her, broke away. He stroked her thighs, her hips, anywhere, everywhere. If he could have engulfed her in fire, he would have. If it was possible, he would have drowned her in silk and gold.

He wrapped her legs around him and took her, not with the gentleness he'd first intended, but with some rick dark emotion so powerful he was drowning in it. He plunged and withdrew, stroked and teased, until her body grew taut and wild beneath his. He saw the fire of want in her eyes. He waited until he saw wonder. When the first crest of pleasure took her, her eyes grew soft, stunned, liquid. He took her higher. This was for Jill. This was about reaching sky, with her, for her. This was about a man who knew damn well he had nothing to give her but this.

She cried out once, wild, sweet, and then cried out again. Release racked his body like the rush and roar of tide, immutable, endless. Pleasure paled next to this. This was a crash of fire and ecstasy, of everything he wanted for Jill.

Breathing heavily, drained, he wrapped her tighter yet and dragged a last kiss on her mouth. He fell back, taking her with him, holding her, holding her.

In time, she felt him stroke her hair, her cheek. She had never felt more small, more fragile, more loved. She heard his fierce low whisper, like a cry of despair, "How am I ever going to be able to let you go?"

She gave him the only answer she had. "I love you, Treveran."

If he didn't respond that instant, Jill didn't mind. Telling him was its own joy.

"Okay, what now?"

Jill stuck a finger in the dandelion, lemon, orange and sugar mixture. It had finally cooled. "Dissolve the package of yeast and a teaspoonful of sugar in a cup of warm water."

After a moment, Grey said, "Done. Now what?"

"Add the half pound of raisins."

"Done."

"Now we mix the whole thing together, pour it in a gallon jug, and you've made your first dandelion wine. After two weeks, it has to be skimmed, strained, rebottled, but there's nothing else to do now. Except..." Jill snapped her fingers and hurried over to the kitchen drawer. A hammer landed on the counter, then rubber bands, four screwdrivers, a lipstick, two hair bands, shoelaces and seven scratch pads. "Aha!" Her fingers emerged triumphantly waving a balloon.

"Do you also have emergency elephants in that drawer?" he asked mildly.

"Pardon?"

"Never mind. Just tell me why we need a balloon."

"To put over the top of the jug, silly. We don't want the brew to explode when the yeast starts working."

"Of course we don't. How foolish of me not to realize we needed a balloon." Grey shook his head in mock disgust.

"Treveran?"

"Hmm?"

"I can't pour it if you're going to continue to stare at me," she said patiently.

"Was I looking at you?"

"You've been staring at me all morning."

"I have?"

She nodded. "Like a housewife let loose at a sale. Like a banker when he opens the vault. Like a kid looking at a sucker. We're talking rampant lust."

"You're talking rampant egotism. What on earth would a man want with a barefoot woman wearing an apron who smells like oranges and sugar and dandelions?"

"I have no idea. That's what's worrying me." She pointed a wooden spoon at him. "Actually, I know what's wrong with you."

"What?"

"I hate to be the one to tell you this, but you're happy."

Her tone was not only sassy but smug, which was why he hooked a hand on her wrist as she was trying to fly past. Lifting her arms to his shoulders, he kissed her mouth, because it was sticky, then kissed her throat, because it was white, bare and vulnerable.

In due course, the spoon she held clattered on the floor. Jill wound her arms around Grey's neck and closed her eyes. Sensations shimmered through her like warm rain. His wayward grin disappeared. He took her mouth with a lover's intimacy. His hands deliberately slid over her with a lover's special knowledge of what enticed, aroused, excited her. She yielded her mouth with a lover's trust.

Last night—several times—Grey had proven that he was a difficult man to please. He wasn't happy until she melted like butter, abandoned all rational sense and released her most wanton fantasies. Grey had been intent on making sure her old nightmares were permanently erased.

Of course he couldn't. The battering she'd taken from her ex-husband wasn't something she could forget, and memories of that magnitude could never disappear in a single night. Fears hadn't mattered less. Loving Grey had simply mattered more. A cold, lost man had given and given.

Every time he'd kissed her this morning, he was still giving. He'd been kissing her every fifteen minutes. She wasn't getting a thing done.

"Stop that," Grey murmured.

"Stop what?"

"You can't kiss and smile at the same time."

"Honestly, Grey. Those are the best kind. Didn't you know that?"

Not answering, he lifted his mouth bare inches, just far enough so his eyes could possessively roam her features—the faint tremor of her lips, the hectic color on her cheeks, the wicked glow in her eyes. Her old-fashioned apron was sliding off one shoulder. Her hair was flying around her face.

She terrified him.

When they'd first gone outside last night, he'd had no intention of making love with her. Something had simply snapped when she'd started trembling, something that had made honor and common sense and an awareness of his own problems disappear. It hadn't mattered that he knew he was the wrong man, maybe even the last man, who should be involved with Jill. He had to show her how precious and beautiful and special he found her. He'd wanted to erase all her bad memories. He'd wanted to take every fear she'd ever had—about love, about sex, about life—and handle it for her. All he'd wanted was to help Jill because she was the one who'd helped him.

All this time, all these years, he'd believed himself a decent lover. Good sex took a man experienced enough to exercise control, sensitivity and patience for a woman's needs.

All this time he'd been wrong. Good loving took Jill.

After they'd made love the first time, he'd finally gotten her to talk about the night when her ex-husband had attacked her. She'd described a man in a rage, a man who'd lost everything that had ever mattered to him, a man who'd lost all sense of self and was looking for someone to blame.

"I know what a psychiatrist would have said about him, Grey, but a psychiatrist wasn't there. I was. Alone," she'd said helplessly. "I thought he was going to kill me. He was bigger than I was, and there was nothing I could do to protect myself...except shut off, on the inside. Shut out the terror, shut out all feeling, protect myself by withdrawing into this little corner of my head where nothing could hurt me."

Jill didn't blame him, because she couldn't blame a man incapable of being responsible for his actions. Grey saw it differently. In fact, he saw endless potential in a shotgun and her ex-husband in the same room.

But when he'd reached for Jill the second time, and the third time, emotions of fire had turned into emotions of loving, wonder, softness. She'd made love with her emotions laid bare and a naked vulnerability that took his breath away.

Until he'd met her, his entire life had been antiseptic, divided neatly into black and white compartments of right and wrong. Jill rocked all that from here to hell. Jill was color. Jill picked mountains of dandelions, made syrup of violets, swam naked. She didn't listen. She upset him. She made him laugh. She'd also been through sheer hell, yet she never saw giving as a risk but as a triumph and a joy.

She'd shaken him and badly, and she was still shaking him. He'd never expected to wake up to his white witch smiling, high on life, exhilaratingly light-hearted . . . demanding to make dandelion wine.

"Grey . . ." She'd developed a recent habit of talking with the tips of her breasts barely grazing his chest, as if she knew it drove him mad. "I have something extremely important to tell you."

"What?" He'd kill pythons for her. Hell, he'd make dandelion wine on a daily basis.

"You have sugar in your hair."

She sounded smug again. The woman simply gave him no choices. He had to kiss her.

The river ebbed and flowed around them, catching starlight and swallowing it. Itty-bitty waves flip-flopped against the sides of the houseboat. The top deck had cooled after the sunset. Jill had brought up blankets as soon as they finished dinner.

It had been her idea to take out the houseboat. Neighbors had been in a mood to visit all afternoon. She wanted Grey alone.

There was no moon. Stars streaked across the sky like silver confetti on black velvet. Grey was lying on the blanket next to her, arms behind his head, as sated from dinner as she was. He was wearing nothing more than his cast and a pair of cutoff khakis. His shoulders had a fresh coat of sunlight, and contentment reeked from him. She never thought it would happen. He was relaxed from the inside out—at least until she poked him.

"You're not trying hard enough," she scolded.

"I am, too." With all due gravity for the serious game being played, he squinted at the stars again. "I see a triangle."

"I see a field of wildflowers glistening silver in the wind after a rain."

"I see . . ." He looked harder. "A tall building."

"I see an old man in a top hat with fat cheeks and a twinkling smile."

Grey gave up. "I think you'd better give up on me, honey. All I really see are stars," he said wryly.

"You just need practice," she assured him, and snuggled closer, using his shoulder for a pillow, his arms for warmth. "The magic's up there. You just have to quit thinking in terms of solar systems and start thinking in terms of moonbeams. I'm going to teach you to be frivolous if it's the last thing I do."

He already knew that while the stars were not magic, she was. He smoothed back her hair, memorizing her profile, the texture of her skin, her shape. No one had eyes like Jill. No one had fingers, a nose, pale arched brows like Jill. He'd told himself a thousand times how impossible loving her, being with her was.

And he suddenly couldn't stop thinking that being involved with her was unforgivably selfish. He had nothing to offer her until he sorted out his own life. He had never had anything to give Jill, not in proportion to what she'd given him.

For long moments Jill watched the play of emotions on his face, and then she touched his cheek and said gently, "Don't worry about it, Grey."

"Worry about what?"

"About your having to leave. From the beginning, I knew—and so did you—that you were always going to have to leave at some time."

"I know nothing. Except that if I were a better man, I would have had the strength to stay out of your life." He propped himself up on an elbow, feeling half swallowed by the need to protect her. He whispered, "I'd give you your damn stars if I could, you know."

"You think you haven't?"

His eyes were full of sudden impatience. "I think what I've done is potentially hurt you. I knew from the beginning I was in no position to offer you any kind of commitment."

"Did I ask for one?" Her fingertip caressed the shape of his bottom lip. "It was my choice to become involved, not just yours. All I did was to take a small risk, to take in a stranger, to give him a little love and caring." She smiled. "Don't you really see what you've given me back by taking that risk? I was there, last night, when you made love to me. I know what you feel, Grey. You don't have to say it or even think it. You gave me love—lots, eons, milleniums worth. And your having to leave at some point couldn't, doesn't, and will never change that." A frown etched her brow when he abruptly loomed over her, all grave shadowed features and a mouth set in a determined line. "Go ahead. Try and argue with me, Treveran."

Her mouth was as sweet, as tender, as vulnerable as her violets. "I learned a long time ago that there's no point in arguing with you, honey." After another butterfly kiss he sealed his mouth on hers, drawing her over him, around him. She was both right and wrong, his lady of the love potions and violets. He felt again, because of her. He loved again, because she refused to give him the choice not to.

But in another world, another arena, a little boy had still died, and in a way that he couldn't be absolutely sure he wasn't responsible.

The night closed over them, ominous, black, shadowed. They weren't Jill's shadows, just his. Making love to her, he banished them for a little longer. For her, he wanted sunshine. For her, he wanted to believe in love just as she knew it. For Jill, he wanted magic.

Eight

The wild huckleberries were smaller than buckshot and sweeter than nectar. As she leaned against the porch support, Jill's fingers kept mindlessly dipping in the bowl, but her gaze was trained on the yard.

Sun streamed on Grey's bare, golden back. His muscles rippled every time he brought down the ax. The woodpile next to him was stacked perfectly and already man high.

The woodpile wasn't the only chore Grey had taken on this last week. He'd oiled hinges, rechinked logs, and painted a wood sealer on the porch floor. New shelves hung in her kitchen, and he'd spent one long day at the dock, refitting and nailing down boards.

Every time Jill heard the crack of an ax or the pound of a hammer, she felt a leaden sinking in her heart. She knew what he was doing—fixing everything he could fix, repairing everything he could repair, all in preparation for his leaving.

The ax blade glinted in the sun, then cleanly split a log in two. Grey wiped his forehead on his arm, then centered another log on the fallen stump. Sweat gleamed on his skin as slick as oil. Less than five weeks ago he'd been pale, gaunt and hollow with an exhaustion that had been emotional as well as physical. Every muscle in his body was honed now. His skin was darker than honey and a vital natural energy radiated from him. She thought about wanting him, then tried to keep her mind on the job at hand.

Anything was easier to think about than his leaving.

"Hey. You in the screaming yellow shorts and the bare feet. How's the soap going?"

Leaning on the ax handle, chest heaving, he glinted at her with dark sexy eyes. "Soap making's done for the day," Jill affirmed.

"Then come over here."

"That sounds suspiciously like a caveman command to me."

"It is."

"I don't put up with that kind of nonsense from anyone, Treveran. Next thing you know, you're going to expect to be waited on hand and foot, dinner on the table, shirts ironed." Her tone disgusted, she ambled off the porch, glared at him the entire width of the woodpile, and dented the progress of womens' lib for all time when she threw her arms around his neck. "Hi," she murmured.

"Hi back." He tossed the ax down. She saw the grin in his eyes before swift, possessive, potent, his lips claimed hers. "Your mouth is all blue," he murmured.

"So's yours, now."

"The berries are sweet. Not half as sweet as you, but not bad."

"I'd say thank you but your judgment isn't worth much. We both know you turn on for the flip of a dime."

He grinned. "What do you expect when you don't own a pair of shorts that cover half your fanny?" He dropped one last lingering kiss on her lips and then leaned over to stack the last of the logs.

"My shorts are perfectly decent!" She started collecting wood chips in an old sap bucket.

"So's your fanny. If you would like me to go into intimate detail—"

"Grey!"

Chuckling, he pushed the last log in place and changed the subject. "Break time. And I have plans for you—a Treveran-cooked dinner, followed by a Treveran-supervised nap for the lady who's been working like a devil all week, followed by a swim in the creek."

"Sounds good, except for the last part. Did you forget your cast?"

He said carefully, "I haven't forgotten it. It's simply time it was taken off."

Jill's eyes zipped up to his. "Grey, it's too soon. *Way* too soon."

He finished sweeping the wood scraps in the bucket, all the while avoiding her eyes. It wasn't too soon to take off the cast. In fact, there were only two reasons he was still wearing it. One was because of the amount of heavy work he'd wanted to do this past week—although his ankle was healed, it could only take so much stress.

The second reason was solely for Jill. Once the cast was off, he knew as well as she that he had no more excuses to stay.

Three hours later, Jill watched him unwrap the tape on his ankle. The carved wooden cast was already lying next to her. She had a lump in her throat.

The last of the day's sun bathed the dock in heat, making the glimmer of cool creek water as tantalizing as torture. Dinner had been rabbit steaks, berries and spring peas from her garden. She hadn't eaten much, and neither had he. She'd tried every diversionary tactic she could think of to talk him out of removing the cast. Grey had been gentle but insistent.

Finally the last of the tape was gone. "It's so white!" She made it sound like an accusation.

"Ugly as sin," Grey agreed calmly. "What can you expect from a limb that hasn't been exposed to sunlight for a month?"

"It doesn't look nearly strong enough to be out of the cast."

"It won't be running the four-minute mile for another few weeks yet, but it's fine."

"How do you know that?" she insisted.

"I know," he said quietly. Jill was crouched at his feet, wearing the two scraps of green she called a bathing suit. Heat glistened on her skin, a diamond drop of moisture was cuddled in her throat. She looked sexy, beautiful and breathtakingly vibrant. She was also being snappy and waspish and difficult to handle, and he'd never loved her more.

"Since when do you think you know so much about medical stuff?" she insisted.

He drew in a breath. Since he'd graduated from medical school, he wanted to tell her, and couldn't. The reason he couldn't was the same reason he could no longer postpone removing the cast. Denying the knowledge he had of medicine increasingly felt like lying to Jill. Allowing himself to continue to think like a doctor felt like lying to himself.

He needed a job. He had to make decisions about what he was going to do with his life, and then move on those decisions. He also had to do something about the load of guilt he was carrying for one five-year-old little boy, yet that was only another reason he had to leave.

Jill deserved a whole man with a future, not half a man with a shadowed past. She was hardly going to find that other man while he was sleeping in her bed every night, and inseparable from her half the days.

The only interesting little glitch was that he didn't know how in hell he was going to leave her. The idea of her shaking her finger and looking testy and impatient at any other man made him feel violently ill.

"You know nothing, Treveran. Nothing. That ankle's my baby. *I* fixed it, not you, and you know darn well you have an idiotic tendency to push yourself."

"Yes, ma'am," he said obediently.

"So maybe it won't hurt it to be in the water for a few minutes. But no acrobatics or fancy stuff."

"Yes, ma'am."

"For that matter, if the ankle feels the least weak; if you feel the least pain—"

She obviously wasn't going to let up and she was perched right at the end of the dock. He gave her the slightest nudge and down she went with a major splash.

She came up sputtering, her hair plastered to her scalp, but her brazen grin was back. She shrieked when he dove in after her. He barely surfaced, loving the brace of cold water on his sun-baked skin, before Jill was pushing him down again.

He stole the top and bottom of her suit, chased her around the houseboat, refereed a race between her and Wolf, captured kisses and accepted retribution in due course when both dog and woman ganged up on him.

Twice, Jill lugged him back to the dock with dire threats about resting his ankle. He was dominantly aware of the weakness of his ankle. He was more aware that he wanted this night with Jill, and his mind kept memorizing the small things: the flavor of a languid summer evening, the icy relief of water when the temperature was crushable hot, the laughter floating on a fretful breeze, the sharp greens and the dragon-flies.

The sun went down. The moon came up. All Jill could think of was that she'd never seen Grey like this. He was so full of mischief, and his laughter came so easily. Not for the first time, he disappeared under-water and suddenly emerged in a shaggy splash right in front of her. He pounced and she retreated in a lover's game, in which the ending was as inevitable as moonlight and air. The rub of cold, slick skin, thighs secretly courting each other beneath the surface, the buoyancy of water arousing erotic possibilities that were new, tempting, endless...she neglected to tell him that his lips were blue. So were hers. Who cared?

"You taste different by moonlight," he murmured.

"So do you."

"You taste...delicious."

"So do you." She offered abandoned kisses to his lips, his nose, his shoulder. Her kisses were slightly flavored bittersweet. In the very back of her heart, she couldn't seem to forget the fib she'd told him a cen-tury ago after they'd made love for the first time.

She loved Grey for Grey, and never because she expected a commitment from him. But somehow she'd hoped he'd return her feelings. He was strong again in every way. She knew their life-styles, personalities, even their values were different. The need to protect herself, physically and emotionally, had dominated her life since her divorce. But she didn't now feel that way with Grey. She trusted him as she'd never trusted anyone, and she kept believing he would see what they had together.

"You're shivering," he whispered.

"I don't care."

Grey did. He challenged her to one last race, and when they reached the dock, he lifted her up and watched with a grin as she collapsed, arms flung, spine like jelly, lungs heaving. "You're not tired, are you, Jill?"

"I'm never tired," she reminded him, and raised one lazy eye when he heaved himself onto the dock. "You lost your suit," she mentioned.

"So did you."

"And my favorite," she scolded him. Her tone was muffled; he'd thrown a towel over her head and undoubtedly believed he was doing a gentle job of drying her.

"If you're short on bathing suits, you could borrow one of my handkerchiefs. They'd cover twice as much as that suit did." He rubbed her roughly because she was cold. She was also as pliant as flotsam. He finished drying one of her legs and it dropped back on the deck like dead weight.

It didn't take that long for either of them to warm up. The night was like tepid water, all liquid heat and still. The swim had drained all their excess energy. Grey dropped the towel on the dock and then eased down beside her.

"We'll get a moon tan if we stay out here too long," she murmured. When he didn't answer, she turned her head. "Are you going to sleep on me?"

"No." He laced his fingers with her, pressed. "I was just thinking that this was a perfect place—the trees, the water, moonlight. And that you seem incomparably happy here. You never miss city life, Jill?"

"Yes and no." Because his voice was quiet and thoughtful, she turned more serious, too. "I don't miss upwardly mobile and rat-race schedules, but heaven knows, I miss washing machines and electricity." She adjusted the towel behind her head to make a pillow. "Still, this area isn't going to be a wilderness forever. It's on the edge of transition even now. Truant officers are going to catch up with the kids; the phone company stops for no man."

"And you hate that idea?"

She hesitated. "Not exactly. Fears and superstitions will die out with education, as they should. But I can't deny that I feel a special draw to Gran's land and my neighbors. People clinging to the wrong things because of pride are always the most vulnerable. I know. I've had the wrong kind of pride. I know what it's like to cling to a lost cause."

"Your ex-husband," he said quietly.

"Yes." Her voice turned pensive. "Never mind what happened with him. It hurt long before that because I couldn't help someone who needed help so badly. You may make fun of my marigolds and love potions, Grey, but I feel that I make a difference here. Maybe it adds up to nothing. All I can see is that if the

IRS and welfare agencies and truant officers swoop down on this area en masse, people's self-respect and pride will be hurt. It doesn't have to be that way, if someone will take the patience and time."

He leaned toward her, stroking her cheek. "I wasn't making fun of your love potions and your marigolds, but, honey...you were a nutritionist. You helped people in that job, too."

"Not like this. Not personally, one on one." She looked into his grave, dark eyes. "I don't pretend to have answers for the future set in granite. Obviously I can't stay here if I can't make a go of my herbal business. I care about this area, yes, but dozens of things could affect my ability to settle on a really permanent basis. All I know is that I'll make compromises depending on the choices I have." Abruptly she spun away from the stroke of his finger on her cheek. She lurched up to a sitting position and wrapped her arms around her knees. "Damn it, Grey, why don't you just ask me what's really on your mind?"

Jill rarely swore, and never turned tense and taut at the flip of a switch. Alarm pulsed through him. "I thought I was."

"No, you weren't. We've done this before. We talk about me, never you. And even when we talk about me, you stop at a certain point. You come that close to the river, but you never jump in."

"I don't know what you mean."

She whispered, "Risk it, Grey. Ask me. Ask me to go with you, be with you."

Seconds ticked by. An invisible fist clenched in his stomach and he felt pain coming in waves—her pain. That he'd caused. "I love you." There seemed nothing else he could say.

"Then ask me."

"I can't."

"Because of some mistake you made—and yes, I remember that little hint from a zillion nights ago." Her voice was desperate, angry. "Grey, I've already been through hell and back. I know the kind of mistakes people can make. You can't possibly believe whatever you've done could ever make a difference as to how I feel about you, and damn it, you love me. I know you do!"

"It's not that simple."

"Yes, it is."

He drew in a breath. "Jill, it isn't. And whether you believe it or not, the only reason I'm leaving you—the only reason I could leave you—is because of loving you."

She knew he believed what he said. She could see tenderness, yearning, desire in his face, and she knew Grey loved her. It showed in everything he did and said. It showed every time they made love. And it showed now, but so did a bleak, anguished darkness in his eyes that was its own message. He wasn't going to ask her to be part of his life.

Pain and hurt slammed through her like the slice of a knife. Mindless and fast, she gathered her towels and clothes and stood up. "I regret nothing I've ever done with you and I never will," she said softly. "But you either love someone enough to take the risk or you don't, Grey.''

For the first time since she'd met Grey, she walked away from him.

He didn't call out.

She was so sure—so positive—that he would.

Halfway along the path home, her eyes brimmed with tears.

The night was still pitch black at four in the morning. Jill wasn't sleeping when she heard the sound of a booted footstep outside her door. It wasn't and couldn't be Grey—she'd heard him tossing and turning all night just as she had.

She bolted to a sitting position even before she heard the knock. The rapping was made in token politeness. Her door was half open. The light of a lantern momentarily blinded her, but even half blind she could see the shadow was hatted, short and wizened. ''Jill, what does it take to wake you, damn it?''

''Root?'' She grabbed the quilt to wrap around her. ''What on earth are you doing here? You scared me half out of my wits!''

''Git some clothes on, would you? We got trouble.''

''What trouble?'' she started to ask, but Root had taken his light and already disappeared. She stubbed her toe on the bed edge as she flew to find clothes. She tugged on jeans and was still pulling on a striped pullover as she hurried from the room, guessing where

Root was from the lantern shadows flickering from the kitchen.

"What in heaven is wrong?" she demanded. Root looked as weary and impatient as she felt. Purple half-moons cradled his eyes and he was hugging the hip that gave him rheumatism trouble.

"Tom Parker woke me a half hour ago, half out of his mind. You know Sue Ellen?"

"No."

"You must know Sue Ellen," Root insisted. "She just lives three miles down river. She's been Faith's bosom friend for a decade."

"I don't know everyone who lives around here," Jill said impatiently. "What's the difference if I know her or not?"

"She's having a baby."

"That Sue Ellen. I've heard she was pregnant."

"Well, she's past pregnant now. She's having the baby, only it ain't happenin' right. It's her fifth, see; she ought to know. She and Tom ain't much on doctors since her sister lost a child to a doctor in Poke Creek. That was hardly a problem anyway, since they lined up a midwife, but Tom says she's been in labor all day and the midwife can't be found for love nor money. He says Sue Ellen's in trouble and she's gotta have some help."

She shook her head fiercely. "But I'd be the last person who could help her, Root. You know that. Having a baby isn't something like fixing a cut or a bit of a sprain. I don't know anything about midwifing."

"Can't ain't worth a strip of grass, Jill. There wasn't nobody to ask but you."

Her head felt fuzzy and embers of anxiety were settling in her stomach. Too many hours without sleep were catching up with her. "I'm the last person who could help her," she repeated, and pushed at her hair, trying to think. "Couldn't Tom take his wife downstream to Poke Creek or Raider's Cove? Is a boat a problem? Or are they worried about someone to watch their kids, or if they just want someone to fetch help for them—"

Root said patiently, "It's too late for all that, Jill. She ain't in no shape to take nowhere."

Jill bit her lip. "All right, and darn it, we'll get help for her, but not me. There has to be someone around who knows something. What about Faith? She's had a zillion babies."

"Shore, Faith could help. But she's another three miles south and by land, which adds up to another six miles round trip. Tom says Sue Ellen ain't got that kind of time. Now I don't know what the Sam Hill we're standing around here dithering for. I sure ain't goin' back there without you, and you know—" Root stopped talking abruptly.

"Exactly how long will it take us to get there?"

The flat, harsh voice behind her couldn't have startled her more. Jill's head whirled around. Grey was standing in the doorway barefoot, shirtless, his hair still tousled. Confusion seemed to affect the flow of blood to her head. The man she'd left at the creek— the man who had cost her one long heartache of a night—wasn't this man. Grey's head was thrown back, arrogant and tense, and a man in a rage couldn't have colder, blacker eyes.

He looked at her, once, a tick of a second when she saw something else—a flash of tenderness in his eyes, so naked and soft and intense that it took her breath away. But maybe that was something she just wanted to see. The Lord knew, in the next second all hell broke loose. Grey was pelting out sharp orders and all three of them went in motion.

There wasn't another soul on the river. Root was driving the boat like a bat out of hell, and the motor was revved to a roar that made conversation impossible. That was just as well. Grey was in no mood to talk.

Jill was huddled on a cushion in the back, her eyes closed against the slash of wind and her hair flying every which way. Every time Grey looked at her, he felt the same slam in the gut he'd felt when she'd walked away from him at the creek.

He'd felt rage at her then, and he felt rage now. Rage at Jill, rage at himself, rage at a river, rage at the old man. Hell, rage at God. He'd been groggy with exhaustion when he'd walked through the kitchen doorway at the cabin, saw Jill's pale face and heard her fierce, panicked voice say, "Root, I can't."

He hadn't reacted to the situation; he'd reacted to Jill. He hadn't thought about an unknown woman then. He hadn't thought about medicine and doctoring. What had mattered was that Jill had been shaken and upset. He'd already hurt her, already failed her. With one exception, he would have done anything to make that up to her.

Adrenaline pumped through Grey's bloodstream as Root slowed the motor to a putter. Shadows relentlessly turned into a shoreline. Every muscle in Grey's body was spring tight and his fingers were cold like steel. No. His head was jammed with the word; his pulse was jammed with all the emotion that the word implied.

"Git the ropes, Jill!"

Root's barked yell was unnecessary. Jill was already standing with the rope in her hands, balancing against the side of the boat as they neared a narrow dock. Grey also lurched to his feet, though God knew why. The dock ended in a stone shore and immediate rocky incline. He wasn't going up there. From somewhere at the dense wooded top, he could see the faint flicker of light. He wasn't going up there, either.

He'd already been through this. Exactly this. The taste of gunmetal in his mouth was as familiar as if it had all been yesterday. The night with the boy, his judgment had been as clouded by predawn exhaustion as it was now. Like the boy, the pregnant woman apparently hadn't received any medical attention until her condition had reached trauma proportions. And he could feel the dread of helplessness clawing at the stone in his chest, exactly as he could on that other night.

He was not going to watch another human being die. He was not going to take that rage of responsibility for anyone's life again.

Jill still had the mooring rope in her hand when Grey barreled out of the boat, pelted down the dock and headed for the incline. She threw the rope to Root, ignored whatever he was trying to yell at her and surged after Grey.

A stone lodged in her shoe as soon as she took the first step up the hill. The stone hurt, and she briefly considered a good, solid scream. Nothing had made logical sense since Grey had abruptly taken charge at the cabin...and nothing had made emotional sense for Jill since he'd let her walk away from him at the creek. A scream seemed an excellent way to vent a major case of bewilderment, worry, hurt, anxiety and frustration.

Unfortunately, there wasn't time. She shook out the stone, jammed the shoe back on and huffed up the incline. The damn fool didn't seem to remember he had a marshmallow ankle. Grey was crashing far ahead of her at racecourse speeds. Like him, she didn't need a map to know where she was going. The only lights around came from the peeling white two-story farmhouse.

She saw the dirt yard and old, weathered farm buildings. Poverty was only emphasized by a single bedraggled petunia that sat in a clay pot on the sagging porch.

A chicken skittered out of Grey's path—luckily for the chicken—which was when she finally caught up with him.

"Grey!" she cried. Out of breath and winded, she grabbed his arm. "You don't have a cast, you don't have a cane, and that's *my* ankle you're treating like a piece of forgotten baggage. Now ease up! Thirty seconds can't make that much of a difference, and if you go in there with a scowl like that, you'll scare the baby out of the poor woman."

He didn't seem to hear her at first, but then he suddenly seemed to realize she was there. Fiercely, harshly, his hands gripped her shoulders as if he wanted to shake her. "I not only love you, Jill Stanton, I adore you. And the only reason I let you walk away from me at the creek was because of this—because I can't go in there and deliver that baby."

Jill saw something inexplicably soft in Grey's rage. A dawn-lit farmyard disappeared. For those few seconds, there were only the two of them. She had no way to understand the emotional undercurrents that scored his words, but she didn't immediately need to. She understood what mattered. He loved her and the risk he'd been afraid of taking was somehow here, now, tied up with a woman neither of them had ever met. His eyes were black and bleak in his pain.

"You don't think you can go in there?" she murmured gently. "Funny, but you nearly mowed down that hill getting this far. Something tells me that Sue Ellen Parker couldn't be in better hands."

"I'm not a doctor. Not any more." Raw, helpless, he heaved out, "A child died because of me."

Her mind started clicking, a dozen things making sense all at once. But there wasn't time for conscious thought, and certainly she didn't need to think to answer him. "No, he didn't."

"You don't know—"

"Of course I know. I know you. I took care of you when you were in so much pain you couldn't move; I know how you think, I know how you make love, I know how you tie your shoes. I know you," she repeated. She lifted on tiptoes to push at his hair. After the boat ride, his hair looked more rumpled than if he'd just climbed out of bed. She suddenly desperately wished he had. Hers. "If that was what all the guilt and nightmares were about, Treveran, remind me to kick you as soon as we get home."

"You're not listening."

"Of course I'm not. No child on this earth was ever hurt because of anything you did. How could you think such a stupid thing?"

"Jill—"

Two of his shirt buttons were undone. Impatiently, she straightened, buttoned, fussed, needing the contact, love flowing from her fingertips to the exact point of touch. It was all she could give him. "You care from the soul about people, dearie dumps. Didn't you know? You take on other people's hurts so hard that you hurt. I should know. You took on mine. You'd probably take on responsibility for the whole damn world if someone let you. And in the meantime, this is a pretty silly time to discuss what an idiot you are.''

She knew he'd stopped listening, because his gaze kept darting toward the house. Seconds ticked by, one, two, three. ''Grey—'' She knew there was a hint of desperation in her voice.

His smile was sudden and startlingly intimate. ''Are you through lecturing me, honey? Because last I knew we had a baby to deliver.''

She kissed him, quick, and they climbed the porch steps. If Jill's heart was still hammering in her chest, she didn't want him to know. An awareness of the true guilt and grief he had been carrying around made her want to hold him for the next four years, nonstop, no breaks for eating and sleeping. She wanted to hear the story of the child, and now. She wanted to be there for him.

What she wanted wasn't to be, but what happened was certainly never what she expected. The instant Grey stepped in the farmhouse, all anxiety and indecision dropped from him like unwanted baggage. He walked in with head high and a determined stride, and the first words out of his mouth were calm, quiet and brisk. He had five people at his beck and call within seconds. He seemed to take that for granted, as they did. He was a man to take charge; it showed in his eyes and his posture and the way he moved.

She was unutterably proud of him and also—abruptly—as panicked as she'd ever been in her life.

It wasn't just a troubled household, but a house in the grips of a nightmare. She saw first a huge cluttered kitchen, then a clothes- and toy-laden living room. Bare lights lit every ceiling, illuminating the life of a crowded and struggling-poor family. Four children, a man and his wife were all in a bedroom on the first floor. The littlest ones were wailing and there was a wild, hunted look in Tom Parker's eyes. He'd passed the end of his rope and lost any hope of anything to hold on to.

Jill had seen poverty before, and her whole life she'd taken pride in staying calm in a crisis. It wasn't the house or the children or Tom that shook her, but the look of Sue Ellen in the bed.

Covers were mounded over her rounded stomach, appallingly heavy for the heat. A smell of blood and sickness dominated the small bedroom. Sue Ellen's face was gray, her eyes were closed and she was lying completely motionless.

Something clamped in Jill's throat and wouldn't let go. She was terrified the woman was already dead.

Nine

———

"Jill?"

She had to force her eyes away from Sue Ellen.

"Are you all right, honey?" Grey asked softly.

Maybe it was his voice, maybe it was just the way he looked at her, but abruptly the panic stopped drumming in her ears. How selfish could she get? There was a houseful of people in trouble, Grey couldn't possibly handle it all and here he was thinking about her. "Of course," she said swiftly.

Rustling the children out of there was obviously the first priority. One of them had a runny nose; all of them were exhausted, hungry and scared. Dawn peeked through the windows as she found bowls and cereal and milk. She filled the kitchen sink with water and soap, stacked dishes, told stories and cleaned up spills. Water was already bubbling in a pot on the cracked enamel stove, sterilizing a knife and string, reminding her every time she passed it of the look of the mother in the bedroom.

Grey was in and out of Sue Ellen's room a dozen times, but he was moving even faster than she was. She passed him carrying bowls of water, bedding and once crib pads he stole directly from the clothesline in the yard. He sent Root back to the boat with orders to return to Jill's place and tow back Grey's houseboat. She understood immediately that Sue Ellen's condition was serious—the houseboat was obviously the best means to transport her to a hospital—but she had no time to question him.

Two of the children were still in diapers, and one cried unless she was carried. Jill carried her while mopping up spilled cornflakes, searching for a broom and trying to swipe the counters clean. Tom Parker, banished from his wife's side, followed her around like a puppy.

"He told me I should stay out."

"I think that's probably best," Jill agreed, as she wiped a little one's face.

Tom shoveled a hand through his hair again. "She's going to be all right, isn't she?"

"Of course she is, Tom."

"It ain't like we never been through this before, but nothin' ever happened wrong to Sue Ellen before. I couldn't make it if something happened to Sue Ellen, and I didn't know what to do. She was hurting so bad. I thought she was going to d—''

"Where," Jill asked swiftly, "is your whiskey?"

It was awfully early for hooch, but the big blond man was beside himself. She sent the oldest to the living room with his father, stashed the two youngest back in bed and asked the remaining towheaded urchin with the big blue eyes if she were old enough to feed the chickens yet. It seemed she was. Even more of a miracle, they had chickens, which took the last of the little ones momentarily off Jill's hands and left only a heartful of anxiety to keep her company. How long had they already been there? An hour, maybe two?

"Jill!"

She dropped the broom in her hands and flew for the bedroom door. Tiptoeing in, she noticed a thousand things at once. The stale, sick smell in the room had disappeared, clutter had been pushed aside, and Grey had moved the bed and changed the bedding. Much more relevant, Sue Ellen was very definitely alive. Blond and small-boned, her face was still dominated by pinched lines of pain and weakness, but the horrible gray pallor was gone and she was in motion. Pain motion. Her hands were gripping Grey's so tightly that her knuckles showed white.

"Okay, breathe out, starting right now, easy, slow...slow..." Grey murmured. When the contraction was done, he mopped her brow and smiled at the exhausted mother. "Our baby is alive and well," he said clearly, probably more to Sue Ellen than to Jill. "The little pistol got it in his head that he wanted to turn around when he reached the birth canal. Not very nice of him, was it, Sue Ellen? In fact, I think I'm going to enjoy giving him his first good spanking in very short order."

"Grey, what can I do?" Jill whispered.

He stood up. "I'll be back within two minutes," he promised Sue Ellen, and abruptly steered Jill just outside the door.

He hooked his hands on his hips and sighed with exhaustion, but she could immediately see that his mask of calm wasn't a mask. He was calm, controlled and confident, and he conjured up a fast wisp of a grin just for her. "You doing all right, sweet pea?"

"Me? What does it matter how I'm doing? How's she doing?"

His brows leveled in an even line. "At the moment, Sue Ellen and I differ on a few priorities. All she wants in life is a loaded gun. I expect directed at her husband or me wouldn't make any difference, any man would do. Personally, I have no fondness for firearms. My priorities are more on the line of a fully equipped delivery room, a stethoscope, a fetal monitor, sterile gloves and number-two forceps."

He sighed, kneading the tight muscles at the back of his nape. "I didn't call you in here to hear our list of complaints," he said dryly. "Last time I looked, you were a little shook up. If I didn't steal a minute with you now, I knew there wasn't going to be a chance." He checked himself when he saw the expression on her face. "I didn't mean it like that. It's bad, Jill, but not that bad."

No? She badgered him into explaining and then wished she hadn't. Hospital or not, a Caesarean section would have been Grey's choice for the young mother, six hours ago. They hadn't been here six hours ago, and now it was too late. There would come a point in the natural course of labor when Grey could reach the baby, but he needed the mother's help to get there. Sue Ellen had the instinct to push, but she was out of energy, out of strength and totally exhausted. "Her blood pressure's high and she's too damn weak. Short and sweet, that baby needs to be born within the hour," Grey said quietly.

"Or what, Grey?"

"Or nothing. That's our choice, so that's what's going to happen," he said simply. "Stop worrying, Jill. Worrying won't help. Get yourself a cup of coffee, put your feet up—"

And he'd handle the whole thing alone? "When cows turn green," she informed him, and whisked back in the bedroom ahead of him.

She desperately wanted to help. The only thing she could do was deliver back rubs and sympathy. Jill watched the fierce contractions rack Sue Ellen's body until she felt like crying out with her. Twenty minutes passed, and then another twenty minutes. Every ticking second represented increased danger for the mother, and Jill wasn't sure why or how her feelings of frantic anxiety turned slowly into a soft, sure, growing excitement.

Maybe it was just watching Grey with Sue Ellen. Seeing the man as a doctor was to know the lover in a

completely different dimension. He was so obviously
born to do this. Caring, patience, tenderness poured
out of him in never-ending quantities. When the whole
damn world seemed to be falling apart, he grew
stronger, quieter, more sure. The worst was when Sue
Ellen suddenly panicked, gave up, burst into tears.

"I can't!"

"One more push, and I can reach him, sweetheart.
Bear down one more time..."

"You keep saying one more time! It's never one
more time! I hate you and I hate Tom; I really hate
Tom—my baby's going to die!"

"No, he isn't."

"I'm going to die!"

"There isn't a chance in hell I'm going to let you
die."

For one stark moment, Jill saw anger in his eyes and
all she could think of was yes. A respect and commitment to fight for life was so deeply a part of Grey. She
suddenly had the horrible measure of what it had cost
him to even consider giving up medicine. Then Sue
Ellen screamed, once, a hoarse, helpless cry.

Seconds after that there was an abrupt squall,
piercing and strong. Later, much later, Jill would remember Grey's forehead bathed in sweat, the blood,
the mess, the smells and the mental promise never to
have a child as long as she lived.

But right then there was nothing but that ugly blue
bundle, screaming its perfect tiny head off, bitty toes,
bitty fanny, mounds of matted brown hair... beyond
perfect, beyond beautiful, beyond the awe of won-

der. And Grey had a look on his face. Exhaustion and
hard-core realism transformed into a shameless glow,
a respect for life so immutably sacred. The smile that
came out of his soul and turned into a roar of trium-
phant laughter.

"We have," he announced, "a boy."

"We have," Jill corrected him softly, "magic."

By four that afternoon, Grey was stretched next to
Jill on his bed in the cabin. Sue Ellen, Tom and the
baby had been houseboated downriver. Billy, the oldest Parker child was taking care of the family live-
stock and the three other young ones were camping at
Faith's.

There had been nothing else to do beyond take a fast
bath in the creek. That, too, had been done and thirty-
six hours without sleep were fast catching up with
Grey. Sleep was the only thing on his mind. It should
have been on Jill's.

He looked at her through half-shut eyes. Her hair
was still damp from their creek bath and curling wildly
around her face. Her eyes had violet smudges of exhaustion. She was wearing her favorite night gear, a
cerise T-shirt bright enough to wake the dead. It
clashed with her hair.

She looked beautiful. She'd been bouncy and ec-
static when the baby was born, high as a kite and vibrant all through the last arrangements and
transportation. But a quiet had settled on her now and
her eyes were full of the questions there had been no
time to ask him before.

He gave up trying to sleep and raised an arm. Like swallows to Capistrano, she surged for home, tucking her head against his shoulder, draping her hand across his waist. His lips brushed her forehead.

Kisses weren't about to appease her. "Don't you think it's time you told me about it?" she whispered.

She obviously wasn't going to sleep until he did. The words seeped out slowly at first. Grey wasn't used to talking emotions; he felt more comfortable with facts. The facts were that a child had died under his care on a long-ago night last spring. The facts were that no doctor entered into medicine without understanding that he couldn't save every patient. The facts were that no one had blamed him for the child's death—except Grey himself. The problem for him was just that: facts. He had wanted it in black and white that there was nothing else he could have done, that he had taken every action he could to save the boy. Without knowing that for sure, he'd seen no way to continue practicing medicine.

Before he was halfway through talking, Jill lurched up and knelt beside him, her cat's-green eyes focused intently on his face. "Negligent—is that what you were afraid of, Grey?"

He shook his head. "No." He hesitated. "I must have been through that night a thousand times in my head. I was tired and worn out—but I did my best. That was exactly the problem. Knowing my best wasn't good enough."

"How could you be so hard on yourself?" she said fiercely.

He closed his eyes. "Honey, when a doctor has someone's life in his hands, he has to be hard on himself. He has to be his own toughest judge, his own jury. And a doctor unwilling to face his own limitations doesn't belong anywhere near a patient."

"But this morning, Grey—"

"This morning, push came down to shove," Grey agreed dryly. "Talk about limitations? I was exhausted and my ankle was killing me and I was wrought up—on the inside, the outside, all over. In a sane, rational world, I would never have faced a patient in that condition." He opened his eyes. "It isn't always a sane, rational world."

She smiled. "You're just finding that out?"

"What I found out is that I couldn't walk away. Whether I was good enough didn't matter. Whether I could control all the black-and-white circumstances didn't matter. I could no more have walked away from the woman than stop breathing." He hesitated, and met her eyes squarely. "It's your fault, you know. Until I met you, the issues for me were cut and dried. I believed I was severing myself from medicine because of ethics and integrity. That was a crock, sweet pea. You were the one who showed me I was running away from involvement, from emotional risk."

"Me?" Her forehead wrinkled in surprise. "What did I have to do with anything?"

She really didn't understand. Grey wanted to explain, but somehow the words wouldn't come. He swept her beneath him, never more aware that her skin was cool and soft. She smelled like violets. She tasted like Jill.

He watched her as she suddenly smiled. Afternoon sun. A hot, real, life-affirming sun streamed on the bed. Lovers belonged bare under a sun like that. He slipped off the first sleeve of her T-shirt, then the other.

Desire simmered through him, a fire-hot pulse of need. Not for sex. For Jill. There was a time when he'd thought she was whimsical and impulsive and illogical and irrational. He'd been so damn wrong. Jill was real. Life had thrown her a crippling blow, but she'd come up fighting again, with courage and resilience and caring. It was because of her that he had choices again. It was because of her that he'd found his soul.

He had to tell her the only way he knew how, with his heart on the line.

When his mouth pressed against hers, Jill felt herself sinking, immersed in desperate, passioned kisses and long, strong arms and Grey. The mounds of her breasts swelled for his palms; her skin was sensitized everywhere he touched.

She closed her eyes, aching, and the sensations of weakness and vulnerability pummeled through her, never more powerful. His tongue ravaged her mouth; his hands praised, teased, worshipped her flesh. As a lover, he already knew exactly what to do to make her tremble, but this was more.

He took with the strength of a man who knew exactly what he wanted. He gave with the power of a man who was no longer afraid of his own vulnerability. His kisses consumed. He intended her to feel liquid, boneless, beautiful. She knew he wanted her to feel loved and he made love to her with that kind of desperation, that fierceness, that rage of softness.

She matched each caress, each stroke, each heated kiss. To respond with less than her whole being was never a choice. It had never been a choice with Grey, but the climbing fire inside her was more than desire, more than love.

Mist swam in front of her eyes. He was going to leave her but he didn't know it yet. She knew because of the power and force and strength and richness of emotion he brought to her. He was healed, her so-strong man with the Abe Lincoln eyes. In healing him, she knew damn well she'd lost him. He'd needed her once. Not any more.

Her heart must have always known why Grey induced that dangerous, terrifying feeling of soul-vulnerability inside of her. This once, she did nothing to block the emotion. She offered it freely, like she offered kisses, heat, need, touch, love.

A quiet afternoon in July turned magical. Jill was so desperate to give him everything.

Grey was also desperate to give her everything.

The explosion that took them both had the color of wonder, the texture of ecstasy. Grey held her afterward, trembling as he hadn't known a man could tremble.

Jill held him like treasure, because that was what he was to her.

* * *

"So where's our healing man?"

Standing on the kitchen table, Jill glanced down at Root in the doorway. Hands on his wiry hips, he had his pipe stuck between his teeth and his expression was irritable. "Hand me the scissors, will you?" she asked him.

"What the devil are you doin'?"

She took the scissors from his hand and snipped some string. "You can see what I'm doing: attaching goodies to the ceiling—rosemary, pennyroyal, lavender, sweet woodruff."

"What for?"

"Well..." Jill had her hands full for the moment while she tied. "I could answer that question one of two ways. If you want to talk magic, for instance, the combination of these four herbs is downright terrifying. Lavender represents happiness and fulfillment, pennyroyal has the power to promote inner peace. There's no beating sweet woodruff if you have some personal goal you desperately need success with, and rosemary... rosemary's hopelessly powerful as a love potion. However—" Jill clipped another bit of string with her scissors "—magic not withstanding, I also simply like the smell of all of them, and they make terrific flower arrangements when they're dried."

"That's real nice, Jill. I'm impressed. Now where is he?"

"Gone, as of two days ago," she said simply. "You want some tea? I'll be done in a minute."

"What do you mean, he's gone?" Root dropped on a stool, glaring at her.

"Gone hasn't changed definition. You know what it means, and you don't have to look at me like that, you old coot. There was never any question that he was leaving here."

"I knew he had to return the rental boat. I jest figured he'd be back right after he took care of that."

She shook her head, bundling another group of stems together. "There was never any chance he'd be back 'right after that.' The boat was a nothing detail, for heavens' sake. He had his work in Chicago, his apartment, a thriving practice, everything he'd ever worked for."

"But—"

"How on earth was he ever going to make a living around here?" she said fiercely. "I can't name a soul who could even pay him a nominal doctor's fee. Everything that matters to him is in Chicago. He's close to hospitals with the best of facilities. He could help hundreds more people in a huge city like that than here."

"You trying to tell me he ain't coming back—ever?"

She glanced at her rosemary, pennyroyal, woodruff, lavender. Together, as she'd told Root, the herbs made up the most powerful love potion there was.

Not once, not ever, had she believed in love potions. Gran used to say that magic was nothing more than coaxing a body to believe in what they already believed in. Jill had never believed in magic, just love.

She could have gone with him.

She'd forced him to leave her instead. There simply was no other choice, not if she loved him. He was healed now. He wasn't the same man that she'd found lost and battered in the woods. Everything that had ever mattered to him was in Chicago, and when he went back home he was bound to realize that. Tennessee had been an idyll, containing stolen moments out of time for him. It wasn't his real life. He had every reason to want his real life back now.

She knew what he believed he felt about her, but he'd also met her when he'd desperately needed someone. What if it had never been more than that? And how could he ever be sure, unless he went back to his life free and uncommitted?

His brass ring was in Chicago. All she'd ever had to offer him was love.

She had to let him go.

"He comin' back or ain't he?" Root repeated impatiently.

She strung up the last bit of rosemary, ignored the welling sting of tears in her eyes and climbed down from the table. "I've got a jug of chamomile sun tea on the porch. Come on, I'll fix you some."

The Jeep salesman wondered vaguely why he was bothering. He didn't specifically mind standing in the rain—the August afternoon had been stifling hot with no relief from the hovering city smog until the downpour.

He'd also stood in worse weather conditions to make a sale, but this one was becoming more unlikely by the minute. He'd known the guy wasn't going to buy the minute he'd driven in with a Thunderbird. Thunderbird owners didn't buy Jeeps and this guy just wasn't the hunter or outdoorsy type. His fingernails were too clean, his profile too classy. He'd also talked trading his Thunderbird. No sane human being traded a Thunderbird for a Jeep. Who did this guy think he was kidding?

Grey was thinking along similar lines. He dragged a hand through his dripping hair for the third time. Rain had long since plastered his shirt to his skin. Odd, but he couldn't seem to feel it.

He hadn't seemed to feel anything in the past month and a half. Certainly he'd done things. For one, he'd added Rayburn—the doctor who'd been subbing in his absence—permanently to the practice. He'd also leapt back into full-time medicine without half the qualms or troubles he'd expected. Medicine was his life; it was as simple as that. Expectations that he could save every life no longer existed. What sustained him were the need, desire and dedication to try. It made him more careful, more sensitive to his patients, more mercilessly perceptive to his own limitations. He could not do more. There was also no way he could ever do less again.

Life was good. In fact, nothing had gone wrong in the past month and a half beyond a small problem sleeping. When he opened a window, for instance, there were city smells, not dame's rocket, not sweet woodruff. He was dominantly aware that an occasional shot of Chivas had no remote relationship to the taste of violet wine. Too often when he closed his eyes, he could see the horrible, sticky, deplorable mess it took to make syrup of violets.

She'd made damn clear that she wanted him to leave her.

She wanted to live in her woods, he knew that. Her eyes had been silver-green and clear the afternoon she'd kicked him out of her life, and the reasons had nothing to do with where he lived or where she lived.

For once, Jill had been the logical one and everything she'd said was true. She was usually whimsical to his rational, frivolous to his over-serious, but what she'd said made total sense. Their life-styles and outlook were completely different. They'd met each other in unusual circumstances and built something on mutual needs. Lasting relationships took more than that to make it. She honestly didn't believe they had any kind of future, and wasn't willing to try.

She'd told him to forget her.

He knew damn well she meant it, which made it increasingly difficult for him to understand why he was standing in the pouring rain in a Jeep lot. He knew himself. He was totally incapable of making an impulsive, blind, unjustifiably illogical decision.

"Look, mister," the salesman said wearily, "if you'd get around to making up your mind..."

Jill dipped her head back, rinsing the lemon-lavender shampoo downriver. The instant she heard the buzz of a boat engine in the far distance, she did a fast crawl for the dock, feeling a little irritable. Strangers were not her cup of tea, especially when she'd been skinny-dipping. She surged up to the dock and grabbed a towel.

The towel was barely tucked around her breasts before she saw the gleam of white taking the creek curve. She couldn't make out the pilot, but the skiff was new and powerful enough to be towing a wooden raft behind it. The raft seemed to hold some kind of vehicle. Frowning curiously, she wrapped a second towel around her head turban style, mentally debating if she had time enough to sneak back into her clothes.

"Wolf!" she scolded. The dog's tail was wagging so hard, she was spraying water everywhere. "You're a watchdog," Jill reminded her. "You're mean, ornery, protective about strangers. Remember?"

The dog's tail thumped like a drumroll. The boat's visor still obliterated the identity of the pilot, but gradually she could make out a tall, lean form and mahogany hair whipped up by the wind. Jill made a V of her hands against her forehead, trying to block out the glare of the sun. She saw that the vehicle being towed was a Jeep. She saw the medical sign of a red cross on the side of the boat.

And then she saw Grey.

Wolf pelted off the dock and started to swim for him. She heard Grey abruptly cut the motor and swear. Seconds later, he was leaning over the boat, dragging one bedraggled wet mutt on board with him.

He swore again. She started to laugh and couldn't seem to stop, which was rather an idiotic thing to do when one was diving.

Swimming underwater was fastest. She cut through the current with the speed of 747. When she finally surfaced at the side of the boat, there was a man with Abe Lincoln eyes waiting for her, leaning negligently over the boat's side on his elbows, shaking his head. "My God, you two are crazy. I would have been at the dock in another two minutes."

"Forget that, Treveran. Help me up."

"Not yet."

"What do you mean, not yet?" Vaguely she was aware that her towel was floating downriver. More than that, she was aware that Grey's eyes had a rather unholy gleam. He ducked his chin where he could see more clearly what she was wearing.

"You've neglected underpants again," he mentioned.

"There is a definite possibility that I'm going to drown while you stand there dithering!"

His eyes were full of dance, full of darkness. "I'm sorry, sweet pea—but I need a yes from you about a lot of things before you climb on board."

"Yes to what?" Her feet were treading water like mad.

He motioned vaguely behind him. "The boat's set up to be a kind of floating hospital. The jeep claims to have the power to cut through a jungle; we both know the roads are deplorable around here. And a portable generator's coming, because I don't buy this living without electricity. I've got phone numbers for six companies in Chicago that want your soaps—" He frowned. "You're looking rather excited, Jill."

"Let me up!"

"Nothing in the boat solves a damn thing," he warned her. "I want children. God knows how we're going to afford them."

Funny that her lips were blue when she was suddenly warm from the inside out. "You planning on delivering them?"

"I had that in mind."

"Then I don't see that we have a problem."

He shook his head. "We do. I don't want children out of wedlock."

"This is no time to get fussy—"

"I want my yes."

"Yes!"

"That's better. And if you ever try to send me away again, sweet pea, I swear I'll..." The look in her eyes made him forget whatever he was planning on threatening her with.

He plucked her from the water, bare, dripping, cold. Faster than Jill could draw breath she was wrapped in his arms. Kisses were pelted all over her, one after the other...and then just one, one long one, that made her feel all helpless and vulnerable and loved. Deliciously helpless. Powerfully vulnerable. Sinfully loved.

Maybe it was the rosemary, she thought fleetingly.
Or the violets. One of the love potions had worked.
   Hell's bells.
   Who cared which one?

*   *   *   *   *

Silhouette Desire
COMING NEXT MONTH

#427 ALONG CAME JONES—Dixie Browning
Tallulah Lavender was a pillar of society. Could she throw over a lifetime of dedication to others for a tall, tough rock-slide of a man? She hesitated...then along came Jones!

#428 HE LOVES ME, HE LOVES ME NOT—Katherine Granger
Her book was number one, but Delta Daniels nibbled while she worked—the bestselling diet guru was as fat as a blimp! Enter fitness instructor Kyle Frederick, who aroused other, more compelling appetites....

#429 FORCE OF HABIT—Jacquelyn Lennox
That unprincipled man! Health editor Tara Ross refused to let herself fall for sexy Ethan Boone of Logan Tobacco. Still, she couldn't ignore the spark of passion between them.

#430 TO TAME THE WIND—Sara Chance
Jade Hendricks was as wild and elusive as the animals Russ Blackwell trained. Was his love strong enough to tame her restless heart and set her spirit free?

#431 CAN'T SAY NO—Sherryl Woods
Blake Marshall didn't give Audrey Nelson a chance to say no when he literally swept her off her feet and into his balloon. But would she say yes to love?

#432 MOON OF THE RAVEN—Joyce Thies
The first of three *Tales of the Rising Moon.* One look at ranch foreman Conlan Fox, and Kerry Armstrong knew she'd do anything to win the man of her dreams.

AVAILABLE NOW:

#421 LOVE POTION
Jennifer Greene

#422 ABOUT LAST NIGHT...
Nancy Gramm

#423 HONEYMOON HOTEL
Sally Goldenbaum

#424 FIT TO BE TIED
Joan Johnston

#425 A PLACE IN YOUR HEART
Amanda Lee

#426 TOGETHER AGAIN
Ariel Berk